2 99

NO I

Also by Jan Greenberg

A SEASON IN-BETWEEN

THE ICEBERG AND ITS SHADOW

THE PIG-OUT BLUES

BYE, BYE, MISS AMERICAN PIE

EXERCISES OF THE HEART

NO DRAGONS
TO SLAY

Jan Greenberg

A SUNBURST BOOK

FARRAR, STRAUS AND GIROUX

For Stephen Roxburgh

NO DRAGONS TO SLAY

1

"SIX MONTHS AGO, I got sick. It wasn't a simple matter of taking two aspirins and drinking plenty of chicken soup. Instead, my whole life got turned around. I lost my hair, they pumped my body full of drugs, and most of the time I dragged around like some zombie escaped from Transylvania. It wasn't a nervous condition, so don't think I went bananas and ended up in a loony bin."

Thomas Newman, lounging in his back yard, had to laugh at that line. There'd been times in the last six months when he would have traded places in a minute with some poor crazy. He could see himself shuffling mindlessly up and down empty corridors, doing woodwork and macramé like his grandmother at the senior citizens' center.

What to write about first? Memories pelted him like hailstones. Flinging his pen on the grass, he leaned back in the lawn chair and wiped the sweat off his forehead. Thomas felt lazy, a summer sloth, his skin sticky as if coated with a thin layer of shellac.

August in St. Louis. The end of a long, hot summer. Sometimes a cool breeze would blow from the Mississippi and relieve the oppressive heat, but today the wind only spread the dust.

Usually, he escaped to camp in the north woods of Minnesota, but this summer, except for three weeks that just ended in disaster, he'd been stuck at home. Stuck. Against his will, he thought, ramming his fist through the plastic slat in his lawn chair. It wasn't fair. But then, very little that had happened to him since March could be categorized as fair. Who ever said life was fair, anyway? He slumped down and let the seat slide back until he was almost reclining. The sun blared through gray clouds as he squinted furiously. "Keep a journal," Dr. Myerson advised him. "That may help you sort out your anger." Until today, he'd ignored Dr. Myerson's advice. He didn't want to lapse into a boring confessional or rant and rave about his dumb, rotten luck. But right now his friend Milton Schwartz lay unconscious in the hospital. They didn't know whether he was going to live or die, and Thomas was going nuts waiting for the phone call.

It was strange to think of Milton lying half dead in a hospital room, when it should have been the other way around. That's what made his situation so ironic. Milton dying and Thomas still alive, propped in a lawn chair with a pitcher of lemonade and a notebook, attempting to sort out his feelings. He brushed a fly off his loose-leaf notebook and closed his eyes, but the pictures remained, flashing on and off like a slide show.

The calm face of Penny Slater appeared in his mind's eye. He could almost hear her quiet voice prodding him one spring afternoon in English class. Maybe that's when it all began. At least, the first signs that something was out of whack, like a loose brick that, when disturbed, might topple a whole wall.

"You're drifting off again."

Thomas Newman felt his elbow slip off the edge of the desk. His head jerked back involuntarily. At the same time, Penny Slater jabbed him in the arm. "Wake up. He's spotted you." Thomas yawned, swallowing hard. Mr. Bloughart was looking at him. There's no way to stay awake in this class, he thought. Boring material, Bloughart's droning voice, and a hot, stuffy classroom. He wanted to stop listening, to let the thrumming voice drum the material into his brain without having to acknowledge it. Like photosynthesis, a magical process. But his leg ached. He shook it. Probably asleep, like his mind. Bloughart's voice could hypnotize a person right into a coma. Thomas's leg stung in a million places. Pins and needles. Rubbing his hand across his hip, he was vaguely aware of a hard knot. When the bell rang, he stood up and felt his leg buckle. Penny caught his arm. "Hey, watch it," he muttered, shrugging her hand away. She was a nice kid, but every time he turned around, she was staring at him with that dopey grin. Tall and sort of geeky, she had such a full mop of hair that her face seemed tiny and out of proportion.

"I was just helping you so you didn't fall flat on your ass," she answered, offended. "You don't have to get huffy about it." And off she flounced before he could say anything. Girls. As if he had time for them, always asking a lot of nosy questions, but really saying something else with their eyes. What did they want from him? Sometimes he agreed with his friend Pete "the Hulk" Latham that they were good for only one thing.

"Thomas, may I speak to you for a moment?" Bloughart called from his desk. Here it comes, Thomas thought.

> "Now sleeps the crimson petal, now the white . . .
> The firefly wakens: waken thou with me,"

pronounced the teacher, with special emphasis on "waken thou." "I know Mr. Tennyson's immortal lines are supposed to have a soothing effect, but they hardly are intended to render one unconscious."

Thomas rolled his eyes. Why did Bloughart always talk like some weirdo? It would be different if he were trying to be funny, but he used that bullshit all the time.

"My dear fellow, you excel in all your written material, yet I sometimes think you're learning by osmosis, so little effort seems to go into your work." Thomas had heard that line before. It was true that schoolwork came easily—too easily, he supposed, to ever make it a challenge. He could memorize a page of notes in two minutes, although he forgot it as soon as the test was over.

Out of the corner of his eye, he could see his friends Rafferty and Latham clicking their tongues and snickering in the hallway. Behind his back, he gave them the finger.

"Yeah, well, I try, Mr. Bloughart, but I'm not into nineteenth-century poetry."

"Just get into it enough, my boy, to stay awake in my next class, or you'll be politely thrown right out the door." Pursing his lips, Bloughart shuffled his papers to indicate Thomas was dismissed.

As soon as Thomas got through the door, he burst out laughing. Rafferty pounded him on the back as they headed for soccer practice. Forwards on the soccer team, they were due at the field by 3:30. An awesome threesome —Thomas, tall and slender, with a halo of dark curls; Pete "the Hulk" Latham; and Clark Rafferty, an all-American boy, with blond good looks, and so prepped out that Thomas pictured a crocodile stitched on his pink jockey shorts.

During soccer season in the fall, it was Thomas's turn to be big man on campus. After that, he had to wait until the one exhibition game in May and spring field trials for soccer camp. In between, he didn't mind his anonymity at the large high school; in fact, he almost preferred it. How-

ever, today the coach had called a practice session, and
Thomas could hardly wait. To be the center of attention
one more time, back with the team, might chase away his
spring fever. The girls circled in bright clusters in front of
the locker room and bobbed like tulips at the soccer field.
Sally Greensfelder, Gretchen Froelich, Rosie Ross. "I'll
take the tall one with the curls," Thomas heard one of them
say, followed by giggles. Trying to look cool, he gave them
a thumbs-up signal. A few years ago, when he considered
himself the school loner, he would never have had the
nerve to respond. But being on the soccer team had
changed all that.

"Ripe for the plucking, the little beauties," Rafferty
said in mock Bloughart talk. They figured every girl in the
school was after them. Rafferty and the Hulk played baseball, so they were used to the attention. Sauntering with
them, Thomas felt the urge to attack all three girls right
there on the grass. Lately, his daydreams had to do with
charging, tackling girls as if he were engaged in some sexual soccer game. Lunging and grabbing—was he turning
into a pervert? So far, his fantasies outshined his experience. Except for one or two fumbling attempts, at seventeen he was still thinking more about sex than doing it.
He wondered if Latham and Rafferty felt the same way.

Quickly changing into sweat suits, they ran onto the
field and began rolling and passing the soccer ball. Latham
pushed the ball between Thomas's legs. Thomas whipped
to the left and nicked around him to gain possession, but he
couldn't retrieve it. As the Hulk began to race down the
field, Thomas realized that, right now, only one thing was
on his friend's mind—soccer.

"Watch the ball, Newman," shouted Coach Burly. "He
just nutmegged you."

"Nutmeg, Nutmeg," called Latham, his chuckle carrying across the field.

"Okay, you grubby jock," shouted Thomas, and charged after him, girls forgotten. Damn leg still felt numb. Must have strained a muscle.

"Line up in threes," instructed the coach. "Let's practice two-on-one passing and intercepting. Then bunt the ball back and forth. Use your forehead and chest. Keep your eyes open." Thomas and his two friends formed their usual group. They were the best and knew it. Each contributed a different skill to the game—the Hulk's strength and endurance, Rafferty's speed and a strong kick, Thomas's agility and vision. For Thomas, soccer was magical. With his natural flair and an ability to read a game, he could see things developing, realizing before others what was about to happen, what could be made to happen. But sometimes he was so busy watching the ball, a player could sneak into position and move it away. For the rest of the afternoon, he concentrated on keeping his eye out for empty spaces on the green, as well as on the ball. By the time practice was over, he was sweating profusely, his leg still throbbing. Out of breath, Thomas collapsed on the bench and poured a bucket of water over his head.

"What's wrong, Newman?" asked the coach. "You were moving like a lump of clay."

"Don't know," he managed to mumble. "Guess the sun's got to me." He limped off the field.

2

CLARK RAFFERTY caught up with Thomas outside the
locker room. "Hey, man," he said in his keep-up-the-team-
spirit voice, "have a bad day?"

Thomas tried to reply in a casual voice. "Couldn't move
the ball worth a damn. Foot's asleep." He knew better
than to complain too much to Rafferty. It was unspoken
but understood that their friendship began and ended
with soccer. When the season was over, Rafferty switched
back to his country-club set. Yet Thomas liked Rafferty,
envied his effortless way of making friends. In a game,
Rafferty could be counted on to find the hole and open
the central paths for the team to score. Showing off with
fancy dribbling or hogging the ball wasn't his style. According to Rafferty, it wasn't good form to complain or be
out of sorts. Thomas, whose own version of this philosophy
had been drummed into his head by his father, decided to
chalk up the whole fiasco to one of those bad days.

"Everyone has them," Rafferty assured him. But as
Thomas attempted to make a graceful exit, the stabbing
pain in his leg made him stumble. He wondered if he'd
torn a tendon, which would put him out of the game. His
parents would have a fit if he dropped soccer. "Being on
a team is as important as your SAT score if you want to go
to Dartmouth," his father constantly reminded him. His
mother equated being on a team with social success. "I'm
so glad to see you going around with such attractive young
men," she gushed when he brought Latham or Rafferty
home after practice. The implication was that his other
friends were grubby, which was probably true, although he
didn't pay much attention.

There were never many real friends, just a lot of acquaintances that came and went. When he was ten, he teamed up with a kid named Rocky Alewalther from his Cub Scout troop. They liked roaming the fields near the Missouri River and put together a fairly decent collection of flintstones, now in the back of his closet, covered with dust. He hadn't seen Rocky in three years. After that, he'd had a short romance with a group of Pac-Man burnouts at the video-game center. When his father saw his ten-speed parked in front of Push Button Haven three days in a row, he'd grounded Thomas for a week. His parents had certain standards for his behavior, and spacing out on Space Invaders was not one of them. Getting good grades and into a good college, looking neat and presentable—that's all they talked about. And from what he'd heard in the locker room, that's what other parents harped on, too. His were typical suburban parents, no matter what they said.

When Sylvia talked about living in the city, Thomas knew she was fooling herself. She wouldn't even go downtown for dinner, because she was always afraid of being mugged in the streets. During the cold winter months, she and Sam loved their evening stroll down the white sidewalk lined with colonial houses.

When he was a little kid, Thomas remembered nagging them to take him along. "If you're good and keep quiet," his father would tell him. But he would sprint ahead, jumping and making monkey faces until they focused their attention on him. "Just the three of us," his mother became fond of saying. It was true. He'd always been so absorbed in being with them that friends hadn't seemed too important, until now. His parents took their walks alone these days, and he didn't need to tag after them.

Today, after practically passing out on the soccer field, he found himself pulling down his old collection of arrowheads. Sitting on the floor, piling one on top of the other like toy blocks, he tried not to acknowledge the sharp pain in his hip.

Sylvia Newman poked her head through the door. "I heard someone thumping up the stairs, so I figured you were home." There was a hint of reproach in her voice. He usually sat down with her after school, shared a pot of tea, and exchanged amusing anecdotes about their day. He didn't feel like making excuses, so he kept pushing the arrowheads around and avoided her eyes.

"Goodness, I haven't seen those things out in a long time." She was leaning halfway into the room, but he knew she wouldn't come all the way unless he invited her.

He held up a small, gray chip. "Remember this one?"

She took the question as an invitation and sat down on the edge of his bed. "Wasn't that the first flintstone you ever found? We'd gone on a trek near an old coal mine and stopped to rest by a huge tree stump."

He nodded, picturing the surrounding field of black dirt newly washed up after a spring rain. "I'll never forget discovering that pile of flintstones at my feet and asking you what they were." They smiled at each other. "You used your teacher voice and said, 'What do you think happened here?' I racked my brains for a possible explanation." Finally, he'd offered a wild guess. "Maybe an Indian once made arrowheads here." When she nodded, he'd felt that surge of triumph that always came when he pleased her.

They had scoured around and found two more tiny arrowheads. He rubbed his fingers across their smooth surface and tried to imagine an Indian sitting at the edge of a hunting camp, whittling away stone to fashion arrowheads. A strong sense of connection to that long-ago time had overwhelmed him.

Now, sitting on his bedroom floor, turning the chips over in his hands, he had to smile at that vision of himself

—a little kid, proudly displaying his treasures on the kitchen table for every visitor to see. His mother sat there with the same faraway expression on her face.

"Maybe I'll start collecting flintstones again." His mother looked puzzled. She asked, "Now what brought this on? You haven't looked at them in years. Did something happen at school today?" He couldn't stand the way she always zeroed in on his moods. To have someone practically read your mind felt like an intrusion. If he told her his leg hurt, she'd whisk him right off to the doctor.

He shook his head, unable to conceal his irritation. "Can't I sit here and look at my stuff without you nosing around, trying to interpret every move I make? Go try your Socratic dialogue on someone else. Or maybe you think you're Sigmund Freud today."

Sylvia threw her hands in the air. "Pardon me. I didn't mean to pry." Then, with a hurt shrug, she got up, closed the door, and walked off down the hall.

Pressing his fist over his hip as if that gesture might make the lump disappear, Thomas pushed the pile of stones into a corner of his closet and slammed the door.

3

BY THE NEXT WEEK, the pain was so sharp that Thomas finally confessed. When his parents saw the huge lump on his left hip, now the size of a tennis ball, they reacted strangely. Instead of fussing and screaming at him for not telling them sooner, they stood back and regarded him with horror. For the first time, he was scared. Then Sylvia got on the phone and organized doctors' appointments. His father escaped to the office, withdrawing into moody silence. It was the silence that scared Thomas—like the stillness in the air before a rainstorm.

A series of X-rays and conferences with doctors followed. There were hushed meetings from which he was excluded. He had a jumpy feeling of helplessness. It reminded him of his childhood, when he was ruled by people who wouldn't explain their schemes. Now he had to wait again, at the mercy of others, adult experts. At least a kid can throw a tantrum, Thomas brooded, but now I have to behave.

Two days later, when Thomas was admitted to Children's Hospital, his mother tried to soothe him. "Don't worry. It's probably nothing, just an infection or a cyst." But later, when the doctor walked into the hospital room followed by his parents, Thomas anticipated the worst. They came quietly, heads bowed, as if entering a church. He got queasy at the sight of their pale, grim faces. His knee wobbled uncontrollably under the sheets. For three days he'd endured enemas, pinpricks, X-rays, and nosy interns. He'd refused to consider anything serious—pushed back his wildest fantasies. But after the biopsy, when Dr. Myerson sat down on the edge of his bed, squeezed his arm, and began to talk in low, soothing tones, Thomas knew what he'd dreaded all along. He had a tumor—and it was malignant.

"It's a form of cancer, but properly treated . . ." The room blurred, and the words circled his head, buzzing like hornets. Nothing the doctor said seemed to register. Thomas went numb, his mind blank. It wasn't that Thomas didn't believe the man. Yes—he had cancer—he was in for some miserable months, painful medication, and so on and on. Information, facts, figures, details—he heard the names of medicines, the procedures, but felt as if Myerson were talking about someone else. It was like taking a big pill, feeling the bitter taste on his tongue, even swallowing. But he couldn't digest it.

For the next four days, as friends and relatives passed in and out of Thomas's room, he sat up in bed and held court—cheerful, good-humored, a model of what Clark Rafferty would have called "good form." His doctor later termed it a state of euphoria—temporary disbelief. He played the clown and flirted with the nurses, he entertained his father with tales of his sexual exploits and recited T. S. Eliot and Billy Blake for his grandmother. "Tiger! Tiger! burning bright in the forests of the night." When he came to "frame thy fearful symmetry," he lunged out of bed, his white hospital gown flapping, and pranced around her. Grandma pretended to be annoyed. He knew she loved this act, performed so many times for her since he'd memorized the poem in sixth grade. He turned and flashed, flipping his gown to expose his rear end, and then leaped back on the bed.

"Cover yourself before the nurses come in," his grandmother shrieked. "You're a menace." He'd gotten her where he wanted—laughing at his antics. Her little boy-chikla again.

Thomas refused to think about the grim prognosis. "Thirty percent chance," if he let them pump his body full of drugs for the next eighteen months. "Amputation is too radical," he was told. The operation, called a hemipelvectomy, was gruesome and involved removing the whole pelvic area. Myerson didn't recommend it, but Thomas would have vetoed it anyway.

Once he was ready to leave the sterile hospital room, reality began to hit him like slapping waves in a sea storm. He didn't know whether he was sinking or swimming.

4

"THE NEXT EIGHTEEN MONTHS will be hell," Dr. Myerson told him, "but at the end of it, you might have your life back."

Thomas repeated "might," pressing it through his lips into a question, but the word stuck in his throat. What came out sounded more like a hoarse croak. "Might"? No guarantees even after six weeks of radiation and months of drugs whose names he couldn't pronounce. The trip from room 203 down the long corridor, past the nurses' station and X-ray to the elevator, seemed to last forever. A stocky aide pushed him in a wheelchair, with his father walking silently alongside, carrying his canvas suitcase. As the door swung open at the lobby, Thomas sprang from the chair and limped as quickly as he could manage toward the exit, where his mother waited in the car.

"But the rules," protested the orderly.

"I don't care about the stupid rules," muttered Thomas. "The only way I intend to come back and forth to this hospital is straight up."

His mother's forehead was pressed against the steering wheel. When she saw him approach, she lifted her head and smiled, balancing stiffly as if she had a crick in her neck. Thomas was afraid she might burst into tears. He managed a weak grin. "Mom, I'm in great shape. Don't worry." He did a little jig and tried their old standby joke from the days when she taught him to read out of a Dick and Jane book. "See Tommy jump?" Slipping in beside her, he gave her hand a squeeze. "You know what? I've got the same feeling I get before a soccer game and the coach yells, 'Get in there and fight.' " She put her head on his shoulder. "There's an invisible opponent—inside now—but dammit, I'm going to win." Please, he pleaded silently, keep this going. Don't break down.

"I love you," she whispered into his shirt. "I know you'll win. We'll do what we can to help you through this."

He was ready to face going home, doing what had to be done. There was a pile of overdue assignments, and finals to take. He'd resigned himself to the fact that he'd have to drop soccer, which was even more painful than the possibility of repeating a year of school. His father dumped the suitcase in the trunk and pulled his large frame into the back seat.

"I've got to get back to school," Thomas said. "I've been out for two weeks."

Silence. His father cleared his throat and rubbed his palm over his bald head, one of his predictable habits before some pronouncement. "Son, I think you'd better forget about school this quarter. You can make the work up at home and start your senior year in September."

"Why? Why should I stay home? I don't feel that sick." In fact, he wasn't even weak. Except for the pain in his hip, he was fine. "Fine," he repeated out loud.

"We'll see," said his mother. "Wait until you've started the radiation treatments and the medicine. You might be . . ." Her voice trailed off.

"Dammit," he shouted. "I'm going next Monday."

"I know you feel rotten, son. I don't blame you. It's a lousy break," Sam Newman said.

"I'm not feeling rotten," Thomas insisted. "I'm not going to let this change my life. I'll go back to school on Monday and start making up the work I've missed; I'll talk to the coach and see if he can find something for me to do—like keeping score or taking care of the equipment—even if I can't play in September."

His mother drove very fast, as if unaware of stop signs, bumps in the road, or sharp curves.

"Take it easy, Sylvia," ordered his father.

As she slowed the car, every muscle in his body tensed. "What's the matter with you two? God almighty, I'm not immobile yet. Cut this out." He gave his mother a look of appeal. She faced straight ahead, tears running down her cheeks. And it occurred to him he'd been doing this all his life, appealing to his parents, playing the role of a strong, cheerful kid, even when he felt miserable. They'd always hated when he acted up. It made his mother cry, his father angry. When he used to fuss or complain, they would say, "We're too old for you to act like a whining baby."

"Monday's your first day of radiation treatments," his father said firmly. "You're expected there at nine. School can wait. What's important now is to get you well. There are some things we'll all have to put on hold."

"We're postponing our trip to Europe," Sylvia said, "so we can stay home and take care of you."

"I can take care of myself," Thomas said, but he knew he was defeated. He didn't want them to go on a trip. He didn't want to be alone. Not yet. Not until he figured out his new routine.

"Just don't worry about school," came his mother's soft voice. "Concentrate on getting well."

If that's all I think about, Thomas thought, I'll go crazy. He couldn't spend the next eighteen months lying around the house being sick. But what else could he do? Soccer was out. That's all he'd been interested in lately, except for girls. And what girl would want him now?

Suddenly he felt weighed down, as if a stone were pressing against his head. And all he wanted to do was find his way to his room, see its familiar brown walls, his books and records, and crawl into bed.

5

THOMAS HAD BEEN HOME from the hospital for three days, hiding out. His mother kept buying him presents, the kind sick people get—fat novels and chocolate candy. Fresh flowers in pathetic little glass vases appeared on his windowsill. His father, who usually stomped around barking orders, began to move quietly, speaking in whispers. Thomas spent his time puttering and sorting. He'd fixed the screen door, caulked a leaky bathtub, weeded the garden, and washed his car. He'd spoken briefly on the phone to Latham and Rafferty, promised to go over and watch the baseball games, but discouraged their halfhearted attempts to get together. He and his mother kept a patter of inane conversation going. They both knew his radiation treatments started Monday, and neither of them wanted to mention it.

Friday morning, he sat at the breakfast-room table and pushed scrambled eggs and bacon around with his fork until the plate squeaked. His mother offered him orange juice four times. The phone rang. She answered it in the family room, talking in low tones. His father had left for the office earlier than usual.

"Why don't you come with me later," his mother suggested casually. "A young friend of mine, Ana Zacharian, an archaeologist, is trying to stimulate community interest for a project in Illinois. She's an interesting speaker. You might enjoy what she has to say."

"What kind of project?" he asked, although he didn't really care. Anything to keep the chatter going, to prolong another day of puttering and sorting.

"In the summer, she works out of a remote village about

sixty miles from here. It's in the midst of about two thousand prehistoric Indian communities. I took you near there once when you were little to look for flintstones. They're excavating a corn field that's turning out to be one of the most amazing sites in the Midwest."

"I'm not much in the mood for a lecture," he told her. "I studied the Indians in third grade, and that was enough."

"Well, I'm not too excited about that kind of archaeology, either," she admitted. "Sunken treasure or the Pyramids sound more glamorous. But Ana's very enthusiastic about this project. Because we're friends, I've contributed some money. Besides"—she paused—"she's bright and a real beauty."

"Is this called 'Mother's way to get kid out of the doldrums?' " Thomas grinned. "Tempt him with a beautiful lady?"

"Well, the improving-your-mind bit didn't work," his mother retorted, ruffling his hair. "Of course, the alternative might be going to visit Grandma at the Center."

He pushed his seat back in mock protest. "No, I'm coming with you, I'm coming. Maybe I should bring my flintstone collection to show her."

"That won't be necessary." She raised her hand in protest, laughing. "Just get dressed."

"Is it black tie?" And for a moment, with the two of them laughing and joking together in the kitchen on a bright spring morning, everything seemed normal. But by the time they walked into the crowded lecture hall at Washington University, and several friends greeted Sylvia with knowing looks, Thomas had only one reaction. He wanted out of there fast. Squirming in his seat and cursing under his breath, he imagined telling Latham that he'd spent the afternoon in a crowded lecture hall with his mother. Latham would hoot. Thomas wondered if the next eighteen months would find him hanging out with his parents again, spending pointless hours on lonesome Friday afternoons. "Hold on," said Sylvia. "You might enjoy the presentation."

"I know. I know. She's bright and a beauty. You and Dad put a lot of stock in good looks and brains."

"I guess everyone's impressed by that," said his mother, slowly. "Good health we always took for granted."

"Until now," muttered Thomas. Good looks and brains aren't going to get me through cancer, he thought morosely, looking around at the audience, a mixture of students and well-dressed women.

He felt as if all the ladies in the room were staring at them and whispering, "There's poor Sylvia with her sick son."

Right now, he felt ugly and stupid. Sitting there in that stuffy lecture hall waiting for the bright and beautiful Mrs. Zacharian, with all those eyes peering at them, he was getting more and more depressed.

"Sitting here makes my leg ache," he told his mother. "I can't take it anymore. I'll meet you outside." But as he started to slip away, he saw a tall, slender woman make her way down the aisle. She was dressed in bright colors, a flowing skirt and scarf. Hunched over, with long, black hair covering her face, she hurried toward the stage. He watched her as she faced the audience. Her expression was elusive, her arms crossed tightly. She began to speak. Each statement was like an accusation. Unwinding, she paced back and forth. Her voice rose and fell to emphasize her points. Although her delivery was uneven, she affected Thomas like a thunderbolt. He saw image after image flash on the screen—eight thousand years of archaeological history—until she finally presented the last slide, what appeared to be a mound of dirt with a deep trench in the middle and various charred remains on the edge.

"Not too thrilling," said Sylvia, poking him in the ribs. "No gold statues, not even a cracked pot."

"Whereas excavations in Greece bring to light temples, palaces, and tombs with ornate interiors worthy of grand gestures and heroic statements," the lecturer continued, "archaeology in North America seems by comparison like a mere scouring of some minor site—a hilltop encampment of the early Woodland Indians or perhaps some beehive village, yielding nothing more than a heap of domestic utensils and a handful of weapons, few intact and none beautiful."

So what's the point? Thomas thought to himself.

As if reading his mind, she said, "What's our definition of beautiful? Only the palaces of kings? What can we learn from the peasants who tilled the fields, built the palaces, protected the land? That is what the new archaeology is about. We are studying everything we find in relationship to human life. There's no way of telling what lies beneath a brush-covered land, a plowed field, or a tall building. It could be a human culture never before known, a culture whose remains might be a clue to answering the many questions archaeologists have been asking. What today's archaeologists are interested in is not the objects alone but what they can learn from them to help humanity. If we could learn how to prevent wars and how to cope or live with our environment, think how wonderful that would be." She looked around the audience. "And that's why we're rethinking our definition of the word 'beautiful.'" She flipped on the lights, picked up her notes, and proceeded offstage. The people in the audience clapped, gathered their various bundles, and filed out of the hall, chattering about the lecture, heading for some comfortable spot for tea. Thomas was entranced.

"I'd like to meet her, Mother," he said, leaving Sylvia behind in the crowd.

He found her peering in the mirror near the theater entrance. Clicking her heels, she dipped before the mirror like a flamenco dancer.

"Mrs. Zacharian?" The sound of her name broke the silence.

Startled, she interrupted her swirl to face him. "Yes," she answered coolly.

Looking intently at her, Thomas said, "I just wanted to tell you how much I enjoyed your presentation."

"Thank you." She nodded.

His next line would have been, "Good speakers don't instruct, they inspire," but his mother came bearing down on them.

"Ana, darling, you were marvelous," she said. They embraced in a perfunctory way, with fluttery little pecks on the cheeks. "Tommy's been home from school for a few weeks. I knew he'd enjoy your lecture."

He hoped his mother wouldn't continue to explain that he was sick. For the first time, the woman looked at him directly. "Are you interested in archaeology?"

"Not really," he said, "but I used to collect flintstones." He knew he was acting offhand because Sylvia had embarrassed him.

"Ana, I think Tommy would love to hear more about the dig," gushed Sylvia. "Do you have some time to talk to us?"

"I'm in kind of a rush today," she said. "I've got to stop by my office and . . ." Ana hesitated. Perhaps it was the persistent tone in Sylvia's voice that made her say, "Look, why don't you walk across campus with me. We could talk on the way."

At this point, Thomas wanted to put a gag on his mother, but he was still intrigued by Ana Zacharian, so he said firmly, "See you at home, Mother."

Sylvia took the hint and waved a cheery goodbye. He

and Ana walked in silence, passing small hedges which led onto the Commons. Then she said, "Sylvia strikes me as the perfect mother. Seeing her with you reminds me that my icebox is empty and my son has missed his dentist appointment."

"She's all right," he said, trying to keep his tone neutral, but wondering what caused the wry note in her voice. He guessed she was annoyed because Sylvia had been so pushy. Switching the subject, he asked, "When your students ask you what makes one artifact more important than another, what do you tell them?"

"Do you mean do I have a standard, a criterion of judgment?"

"I mean, are they encouraged to form their own ideas? The teachers at my school always seem to want us to feed them back their opinions."

"Well," she said slowly, as if turning the question over in her mind, "archaeology has become a science. So I set up problems for my students to solve, and take into consideration that there are a number of ways to come up with an answer."

"The *right* answer?" He was surprised when she started laughing, wide-mouthed, with a laugh that took over her whole face.

"Is this an interrogation?" She grew serious. "I'd like to talk with you, but right now I need to grab the papers in my office and go home. My son will be back from kindergarten in a few minutes, and I always like to be there." She spoke rapidly, in quick, abrupt sentences.

"I read a book," he persisted, "about a man who takes his son on a motorcycle trip. The journey becomes a metaphor for the search for quality. The author concludes that quality can't be defined. You just know when you find it."

"Yes," she said, an expression of alertness coming into her face. "I feel that way sometimes."

"Read the book if you have time. It's called *Zen and the Art of Motorcycle Maintenance*."

"Oh, yes, I've seen it displayed in the campus bookstore. Well, I'll try." Her brisk tone and quick steps indicated her rush, and she smiled at him with the kind of polite smile that precedes a dismissal. "It was nice to meet you, Tommy."

"I prefer to be called Thomas," he said.

"Well, Thomas"—she held out her hand—"goodbye." Thomas stood for a moment watching her stride away, her purple skirt softly folding around her hips. Then she was gone, disappearing quickly around a corner. He used to be good at charming his parents' friends, especially the women. Yet Ana hadn't seemed impressed. Or maybe he was just being paranoid, expecting more attention from her than he got—expecting her to eye him in a quizzical way, like all the other ladies at the lecture. Was she in a hurry because I said something stupid, or because I'm sick, he wondered. Does she know about me? No, maybe she hasn't heard the latest gossip, he figured bitterly. He imagined people whispering, "Sylvia's kid's got cancer," passed along from ear to ear as in a game of telephone. Sylvia's kid's got cancer, he wanted to hiss after her. That would attract her attention. Oh, to hell with her. What does it matter? What mattered was the awful fact that he couldn't even have a simple conversation anymore without being aware of his disease. He was getting so worked up he started trembling and felt his stomach lurching.

As he walked to the bus stop, he tried to calm down by naming street signs, buildings, whatever he came across. But he felt so frustrated he wanted to smash his fist against a tree. Without thinking, he rammed a mailbox with his foot. The pain ripped through his sore leg and shot right up to his brain. He doubled over, grabbing himself hard around the waist as if to keep from breaking in two.

6

"I'LL DRIVE YOU to the hospital," announced Sylvia on his fifth day of radiation treatments. Every morning it was the same scene—his mother insisting, Thomas refusing.

"Will you cut out the overprotective-mother bit. I'm capable of driving down there by myself." He headed for the garage with her right behind, brandishing the car keys like a dagger.

"You look terrible. I heard you tossing and turning all night."

He swung around to face her. "I don't need a chauffeur-nursemaid. Why do we have to go through this every day? Stop following me around. It's not as if I'm still ten and need to be reminded to take my allergy pills."

"Well, you always used to forget them," his mother retorted.

"I can't forget this so easily." He shook his head. "Now lay off."

Her mouth twitched. He knew he'd touched a nerve and felt guilty for hurting her feelings. But her hovering made him more nervous than he already was about the impending treatment.

She drew a deep breath. "But I know that each day the pain gets worse, and Dr. Myerson suggested . . ."

"I don't care what he suggested. I don't want you sitting in the waiting room like I'm some helpless baby." Her eyes filled. "Don't start crying."

"I'm not," she shrugged helplessly.

"I see tears . . . All right. All right. Let's go, then. I'll drive there."

"And I'll drive back."

He did feel lousy today—too tired to argue anymore. He knew she was right. The surface of the skin on his hip had reddened and blistered, a side effect from the radiation. Every day it got worse—the searing pain, the nausea. But the waiting room at Children's Hospital was depressing enough without having to sit with his mother. "Go shopping," he told her when they pulled into the parking lot.

"I'll be back at 10:30." She checked her watch as if it really mattered that she be back precisely in an hour.

Inside, Thomas glanced around at the pale, bald-headed children, each waiting his or her turn on the big machine; he cringed at the thought of his own hair falling out. Three more weeks of radiation, and then chemotherapy. The oldest patient there, he felt like a big freak surrounded by all the little kids. The boy next to him wore a cowboy hat. He couldn't have been older than eight, his eyes wide and sad, staring down at his feet. A girl pulled at her platinum-blond wig. Soon he'd enter their special club, but he'd be damned if he'd wear a wig. All misfits, all doomed. Osteogenic sarcoma of the ilium was a child's disease. At seventeen, he was a statistic within a statistic.

A slight cramp shot down his leg. Automatically, he wondered if the disease had spread there, too. A flash went through his mind, that his leg would have to be amputated, like the Kennedy kid's. He found himself tearing pages out of an old *Time* magazine in a state of panic. When the nurse called his name, Thomas was grateful to pull himself out of the chair. He limped down the long corridor to the treatment room and removed his slacks and shoes. The technician silently put lead blocks in the slot on the machine. Each patient had his own set of blocks. The radiation would reach only that area designated by the red ink marks on Thomas's pelvis. His scarlet letter. "Lie down on the table," the technician instructed.

"Let's not and say we did," said Thomas, grinning. No response. He'd bantered with him three days in a row, hoping to ease some of the tension, but today he realized that the technician was just doing his job. He could have been working on a computer. He could have been a projectionist in a movie theater. Casually efficient, moving briskly in his crisp, white coat, he smelled faintly of ammonia. Thomas felt like a specimen for a science project—a guinea pig, an amoeba. His body tensed as he gripped the edge of the table. "Don't worry, Thomas, these are the right blocks," the technician told him. Thomas was always nervous they'd use someone else's. You know my name, why don't you tell me yours, he wanted to say as the guy dimmed the lights and left, sealing Thomas in.

A humming noise began. Technician no-name, in a lead-lined control booth, operated the machine while he monitored Thomas on a TV screen. Thomas lay on his side, the nozzle of the machine hovering above him like a large black insect. He imagined being sucked into the snout and disappearing in its whining belly. "Come on, you brute, attack these damn cells," he muttered. His mind drifted as he tried to brace himself against the pain. In two minutes, it was over. The hydraulic doors swung open, and the technician helped him up. "Hell of a way to get a sunburn," Thomas said. The technician nodded sympathetically. God, why did he have to make a glib remark? Was he showing the jerk he was brave?

He could hardly zip his pants today. Underwear was out of the question. The blisters were beginning to ooze. His shirt hung out of his painter's pants, flapping as he hobbled in the direction of Sylvia, who paced the lobby. On the way home, he fought waves of dizziness, his head bent, pressed between his hands, as he listened to her chatter. Although he paid no attention to the words, the rhythm of her voice began to soothe him.

"Thanks for the ride," he told her, as they stumbled into the house. "I just hate making you cart me around."

"I want to help," she said softly.

Sylvia disappeared into her study. Let her spend the rest of the afternoon on the telephone with comforting friends. Now he had to figure out a way to comfort himself. He wrote humorous letters to bunkmates from Camp Thunderbird, announcing cancer casually, the P.S. at the end of the letter. He calculated how long the letters would take to reach Chicago, Minneapolis—how soon he could expect a reply. He felt stupidly delirious. His hip throbbed.

Later, at dinner, he wore drawstring slacks with a hole cut on the side to let the sore dry out. His skin was acutely sensitive to the slightest pressure; even a light dressing hurt. He couldn't think of any other way to keep the raw skin from sticking to the material. His father said, "Why are you flaunting that burned hip? I hope you won't do that when your hair falls out."

"We'll have a wig made," said Sylvia.

"You're bald," Thomas countered. "I don't see you wearing a wig. I'm going to wear my baldness like a crown, like a damn crown."

Maybe he was showing off. Was he a candidate for a Hemingway scar award—noble, received with valor? Job— the suffering Jew. He'd cut the hole in his slacks to be practical, to control his discomfort himself; now his father was putting him down. Why couldn't his old man get off his case? That's all they seemed to talk about—his cancer, their cancer.

Sylvia took a large gulp of wine. They made Thomas feel as if it were his fault he was sick and screwing up their summer.

"I just don't know the social etiquette of this disease yet. Maybe I should write Miss Manners. Anyway, let's not talk about the hair bit until it happens." Thomas bounded from the table, gave his mother a hug, bending around her from the back of her chair. "Cheer up, mamacita, nada." She smiled.

Retreating to his room, he swallowed a pill. Pure marijuana, prescribed by Dr. Myerson to combat nausea and depression. He was only supposed to take one before his treatments, but tonight he felt like getting high. The capsule worked better than the joint he and his buddies once smoked behind the gym at school. At least there's one positive side effect, he thought. As he leaned back in bed, he heard his father come pounding up the stairs. He moved as if he were bursting through a cement wall—head leading, fists forward, stubby legs bent. He crashed onto the landing like a bulldog. As a child, Thomas had been frightened by his father's strength. When he grew to tower over him, Thomas realized that Sam was shorter than most men, but his muscular frame and brusque manner made him appear larger. He had an aggressive clumsiness that Thomas worked hard to overcome in himself. Go away, dammit, he wanted to shout. Stop pestering me.

He waited for the blustering voice to begin. "Your mother tells me the doctor gave you capsules of marijuana," Sam said.

"Yeah, it's supposed to help."

"Maybe you'd better hand them over to me. We'll give you one when you need it."

"I don't think so," said Thomas, trying to keep his voice calm.

"What do you mean, you don't think so?"

"Dr. Myerson gave *me* the prescription. I can handle it myself. I don't need you to regulate my medication." Thomas turned his face to the wall.

"All right, all right," his father conceded. "Just don't abuse the privilege."

"Some privilege," Thomas said glumly. "I'm allowed to get stoned so I won't throw up."

"Look, I know it's rough," his father said, softening. "Maybe you ought to go out with some young people. As a matter of fact . . ."

"What now?" Thomas asked, impatient for his father to clear out.

"Siegfried Schultz wants you to meet his daughter. He's having a dinner party next Thursday night."

"What are you talking about?"

"Sig's one of my best clients. He's made a fortune in soft drinks. He heard about you and thought you might have a lot in common with his daughter. Both of you love to read, and so forth."

Thomas didn't like the sound of that "so forth." He looked at his father darkly. Sam was always nudging him to make plans. Translation—"Get off your ass and out of the house." Hell, the scene might be amusing. The shadow of his father spread through the room like a stain. "Okay, what's her name?" His father beamed.

Thomas tried not to think about the date, but the week passed quickly and then it was Thursday night. He was due at the Schultzes' at 7:30 sharp. Thomas sneaked out before his parents could comment on his tattered cotton slacks. What was the point of buying new clothes now? He put on a thin Mexican shirt, leaving the top buttons open. Very sexy, he told his reflection in the rearview mirror. He drove his old Corvair to tall, wrought-iron gates. The gatekeeper asked to see his invitation and ushered him in immediately. The road wound around the stables. The moon grinned down through the trees. He hummed a soda jingle: "Dr Pepper is the friendly pepper-upper. It never, never lets you down."

Then he was inside, standing at the foot of the wide, pink-marble staircase, watching Bobsie Schultz weave her way down, a smile frozen on her rosy face. She moved awkwardly, Thomas noticed, for a princess. He spotted the bulge on her back and realized she was wearing a shoulder brace. Oh my God, she's a cripple, another of the walking wounded! His father's "so forth" flashed on and off in his mind like a neon sign. They were being pushed together out of pity, out of mutual misery. He tried hard to concentrate on her cool blue eyes, her slightly turned-up nose, and her blond hair. He stifled the urge to say "What the hell happened to you?"

But she was one step ahead of him. "I bet you're wondering why I wear this cage on my back." He started to protest, but she went on in a matter-of-fact voice. "I fell off a horse three years ago during the Bridle Spur Show. I was making a jump. The horse stopped short right before the hurdle, and off I flew—landed on my back. I'm lucky to be walking."

"I'm sorry," he said, steering her toward the dining room. "That was tough." His moment of irritation over, now he wanted to comfort her, to say he knew how she felt. He wondered if she knew why they'd been fixed up.

"It has been tough," she said in that same direct way. "I was in traction, and then a wheelchair for two years. Now I can walk by myself, and I'll be going to college in September. What's your problem?"

"What do you mean?"

"My dad has a habit of fixing me up with retards. The first one was just out of Edgewood—a sixteen-year-old glue sniffer—but his father was Dad's accountant. Then there was one with a stutter, and another whose right eye kept closing."

"That's horrible." Thomas laughed, despite himself.

"So I figured you'd be another winner, too. But," she said, looking him up and down, "except for your twitch, you seem okay."

"I don't have a twitch," said Thomas, wrinkling his nose a few times. "But you're right. I'm definitely eligible for a freak show."

He followed her into the dining room. There were platters of smoked ham and turkey, duck pâté, venison and quail, casseroles of au gratin potatoes, steaming rolls and corn bread on the long table. He reached for a ham sandwich. As far as he could tell, he was the only person present outside the family, except for two wizened old men, who stood at each side of Siggy. Siggy sneezed and blew his nose, roared at the servants, and motioned his sons over to his chair one by one. Thomas and Bobsie were virtually ignored, for which he felt grateful.

"So?" she said. "Tell me about *it*. Besides the obvious 'we have a lot in common' stuff, my dad thinks I'm a good influence."

"You mean 'cause you're so 'well adjusted.' "

"That's me," she said, leading him toward the porch door. "Let's go outside."

"Yes, let's go outside," he echoed, his voice like a snare drum, his hand icy on her arm. Thomas wasn't so sure he wanted to talk about *it*. Later, would she joke about him—the boy with cancer?

They slipped out the door and headed for the lounge chairs, which were spread on the lawn like convalescent beds. Bobsie eased herself down on one chair, Thomas plopped on another and threw off his Top-Siders. It felt good to sit quietly for a while, watching the stars grow brighter, popping on and off like Christmas-tree lights.

Bobsie broke the silence by saying, "You don't have to talk about whatever it is that's happened to you, but I get the feeling you're really uptight. You hold your neck even more stiffly than I do."

"That's to give you the impression I've got my head screwed on right. Any minute it might topple off."

"Oh, so that's your problem. You're about to lose your head."

"Look, I'm not going to sit here and exchange clever remarks with you all night." Then his voice trailed off.

"So?" she persisted.

"All right. If you must know, I've got cancer. Just found out a month ago. Since then I've been having radiation treatments. It's really been tough on my folks."

"Tough on them?" she responded. "What about you? You sound like you're some kind of martyr."

"Well, what am I supposed to do? Yell and scream? Feel sorry for myself all the time?"

"Do you feel sorry for yourself?"

"All the time," he spluttered, and they both started laughing.

"Can you believe this?" Bobsie said. "I saw you standing there—this terrific-looking guy—and I thought, finally Dad's found someone who's not on the rack . . ."

"And now you know I'm the worst case yet." Thomas shook his head, smiling into the dark night. He really liked Bobsie Schultz. She had a sense of humor and wasn't treating him like a terminal case.

"What are you doing with yourself besides being sick?"

"Not much," Thomas had to admit. "What about you?"

"At first, I just lay there and cried. I couldn't believe what was happening to me, Bobsie Schultz, the girl with everything."

"I keep thinking the same thing," said Thomas.

"When they told me I couldn't get out of bed for nine months, I wanted to die. But my family and friends were so worried about me, I knew I couldn't let them down."

"It's amazing how many people call, and send notes," Thomas agreed. "But now things have calmed down, and I have to deal with being sick on my own."

"When you get used to it," said Bobsie, "you'll need

some kind of an outlet, anything to keep yourself sane. I programmed six new computer games and kept a journal while I was practically flat on my back," Bobsie said. "My head was full of notes to myself and mathematical formulas. It kept me sane."

"I should find a project, too, but right now it takes all my energy just to get through radiation. I can't even concentrate on reading a magazine. I keep looking at the pictures."

"I know how you feel. At first I thought every day was my last. Then I decided to live each day as my first. Maybe that sounds corny, but it helped." She paused. "And here I am, the picture of good cheer." A sad look came over her face, and Thomas reached for her hand.

"It doesn't always work," she admitted, "but you have to try."

He couldn't tell how long they sat there talking. One by one the lights in the big house went off until all the chimneys were outlined against the sky, and the building seemed shrouded in darkness against the giant oaks. From the stable came the whinny of a horse; a dog barked in the distance. He found himself growing drowsy.

"Think I'd better go soon," he mumbled.

"I'd help you up," said Bobsie, "but I can hardly move myself." She was propped on her side in an awkward position.

"Are you all right here by yourself?"

"Hey, listen," she said, "you're talking to Miss Independence." She swung her legs over and pulled herself up.

"Bobsie," he said, looking down at her small, curled body, her face shadowed in the dark, "you're terrific." He wanted to tell her he'd call and ask her out, but he knew he wouldn't, felt she really didn't want him to. Bobsie Schultz didn't see herself as an invalid, even if her father did. He knew she wanted to find her own boyfriend, not some cripple, handpicked by her father. "When I get over this, if you're not already married and with a couple of kids," he told her, "I'll call you." And he meant it.

"Sounds good," said Bobsie, "and I hope you do . . . get over this, I mean."

He bent down and kissed her lightly, then crossed the wide lawn, bypassed the house, and turned a corner to get to his car. The grass was a velvet carpet under his bare feet. There was a soaring, buzzing serenade of crickets and night birds. A cool night, sky lit up by stars, and a crescent moon. By all rights, he should have been hopping mad at his father for not being straight with him; instead, he felt light-headed, hopeful, poetical—"the world is charged with the grandeur of God" poetical.

"Glory be to God for dappled things," he shouted to the gatekeeper, who sat nodding off to sleep, as he floored the accelerator and sped down the dark road.

7

"So, how was your big date with the soft-drink heiress?" Sam asked as soon as Thomas staggered into the breakfast room. His mouth felt dry, his eyelids heavy. Ten o'clock. Apparently, his father was going late to the office, waiting around for Thomas to appear. Here it comes, he thought, the third degree. "You must have really tied one on." Slowly, Thomas poured a glass of orange juice and rattled a few plates at the sink. "So?" came his father's voice again.

"We sat around and discussed politics. Then we got

stoned and screwed all night. What do you want me to tell you?" Thomas rasped. Bobsie Schultz had made him feel better, but he wasn't about to admit that to his father.

His father's thick jowls tightened into a scowl, but he didn't pursue the subject. They ate their breakfast in uncomfortable silence, his father attacking his cereal as if it were his last meal, clanging his spoon on the bowl. His eyes darted from the place mat to the ceiling.

"My stomach's upset, Sylvia. Bring me a Maalox," shouted Sam. Sylvia scuttled in, banging cabinet doors, finally producing a small bottle of pills. Then, as if ashamed of this burst of temper, Thomas's father kissed his wife meekly on the cheek, patted his son's arm, and huffed out the door. Just as Thomas's mother was about to scold him, the phone rang. As usual, she dragged the long cord into the other room.

"Yes, yes. I'm sure he'll be delighted you called," he heard her say. Who was she talking to? That Sylvia went on to explain, "Tommy's always been delicate," should have increased his irritation, but he'd overheard that line so many times at family gatherings or over dinner with friends that it had become part of her repertoire, changeless and inevitable, like the dining-room fixture or his grandfather's portrait over her desk. Smiling tentatively, Sylvia handed Thomas the receiver. The voice that came over the phone sounded formal but pleasant.

"Thomas, it's Ana Zacharian. I just found out you've been sick and wanted to tell you I'm thinking of you."

"Thanks. That's nice of you." He mustered an equally pleasant voice. He still remembered his miserable state the last time he saw her. "Have you read the book we talked about?"

"As a matter of fact, I bought it, but I'm afraid I haven't had time to read it yet."

"I'd like to continue our conversation. Can we have

lunch today?" He was surprised at his nerve, felt his face flush and his fingers tingle. But suddenly he had to get out of the house. She was as good an excuse as any.

"Well," she hesitated, "I've got a lot to do today. Two classes and car pool."

"What if we meet somewhere between the university and my house and go on a picnic?" he persisted. "I'll even make sandwiches."

After a moment's silence, she relented. "Okay. That sounds fine. How about Oak Knoll Park at noon?"

"Great. See you then."

He noted his mother's surprised look when he hung up. Would Sylvia be grateful? Is that why Ana agreed to meet him? Don't analyze. Just go, and think about the rest later, Thomas told himself. At the same time, he felt self-conscious, wanted to call back and schedule their meeting for another time. He found her number, dialed seven digits, and hung up.

Packing the picnic lunch in a straw Indian basket, he noticed the simplicity of the design. He could have carried the food in a paper bag, but he wanted everything to be just right—special.

When Thomas reached the corner of Wydown and Big Bend, he sat down on the stone bench to wait. Though it was early May, the trees hadn't fully blossomed. The sun zigzagged through the branches, and pockets of mud formed dark patches on the grass. The thin May air sliced through him. He should have listened to his mother and put on a sweater.

His first impression when he saw her round the corner was that she was a young girl. She moved carefreely. He had difficulty making the connection between the intense professor he remembered and the tall, graceful young woman who now approached him with such an expression of pleasure that he began to smile apologetically. If she noticed when he limped toward her, dragging one foot, she didn't react with the anticipated strained look. Thomas hugged her unexpectedly. The way she pulled back, he could tell she wasn't used to greeting people that way. Neither was he. But somehow he needed to show her how much he appreciated her effort to see him. At this point, a little companionship was more than welcome. He missed being with friends.

Even though his soccer buddies had called a few times, no real attempts had been made to get together. They were too busy with exams or practice; he'd mumbled excuses as well. Sylvia kept telling him to make the first move, but he didn't have the energy. Maybe he was just afraid to face the "Thank God it didn't happen to me" looks.

"Well," she began, "I understand you're out of school for a while. I imagine this whole thing has been quite a jolt." He recognized the professorial, impersonal tone. He'd always felt uncomfortable with sick people, too.

"It happened out of the blue. One minute I was playing soccer, the next lying in a hospital room with cancer. In fact, today's only the third time I've managed to get out of the house, except for dragging myself to the clinic for treatments."

"I'm flattered."

They walked past the stone bus shelter, down Big Bend to Oak Knoll Park in silence. Abruptly, she asked, "How are your parents taking it?"

"Mom's okay. But my father can't cope. Either he escapes to the office or we trip over each other every time I come out of my room. He's never been easy to relate to."

"How many fathers are, when you're young?" she asked, smiling. "Mine was impossible." Ana sighed.

That comment seemed to break the ice. He found himself talking easily all the way to the park. The area was thronged with groups of rowdy schoolchildren. "We're intruders in a landscape reserved for someone else," she said, pointing to the school buses, and to the teachers, who blew shrill whistles and waved their arms like traffic cops.

"There's a quiet corner here where no one will be running around," he said, steering her down the hill through a clump of large fir trees. "I grew up in this park; I know every inch of it." They walked through a clearing in the wooded section, and he motioned for her to sit down. He felt a little nervous and antsy, so he began some stretching exercises, just to unwind. Bending at the waist, hands touching the ground, he swung his legs one at a time back and forth.

"My pelvis is tight," he said. "I've just about finished radiation treatments. They've been doing it in stages, so the tissues around the diseased area aren't destroyed. Next comes chemotherapy. Adriamycin and platinum." He repeated the names of his drugs in a singsong. "It sounds like medical gobbledygook, but knowing the names and what they represent is important to me. In some ways, it makes cancer less of a mystery."

"Yes, I know about that. My son Nicky memorizes lists, a way of controlling all the facts that have bombarded him since his dad and I split. I do, too."

"How long ago was that?" Thomas asked, curious.

"Three years ago. He didn't want me to go back to school to complete my master's degree. But I needed to do my work. He wouldn't help out with Nicky, so . . ." She tilted her chin almost defiantly, but her voice wavered. "It was better to separate before things got worse."

"How old are you?" he asked impulsively, stretching out next to her.

"Twenty-six. Too old for you." She laughed. "Your mother befriended me at a low moment in my life. She heard me lecture at one of her women's groups and began introducing me around." She broke off, pulling a clump of grass and scattering the blades. "This must be hard on her. You're the light of her life."

"She's always thought I was some kind of a boy wonder. Now I'm really a special case."

He told her he'd just read *The Last of the Just* by André Schwarz-Bart, about generations of Jewish men who were chosen by God to endure some great trauma, to perform some defiant act. "Lately I've been feeling that having cancer is some kind of test, a way that I've been singled out. Can you believe that?"

"Oh, that's absurd," she protested quickly.

"Maybe you're right. Maybe I'm being overly dramatic. I guess I'm still asking why, wanting someone or something to blame, looking for a dragon to slay."

"You don't have anything to prove," she said, kindly.

"I guess I want people to tell me how brave I am, but instead I'm finding out that sick people are considered failures." In one of his fantasies, he'd imagined himself walking down a crowded street. People would stop, shake his hand, congratulate him for his courage. But just the opposite happened in real life.

"Shall we eat lunch?" she suggested. He could tell she wanted to change the subject.

The soda can popped, spraying the grass. She spread some cheese on a cracker and handed one to him. Drinking 7-Up and letting her talk about her job and her little boy, he concentrated intently, as if listening to a concert.

"Your voice," he said. "You must have gone to school in the East."

"Oh, yes. Miss Hall's, then Vassar. A proper education for a proper young lady. My father sent me away to boarding school when I was thirteen."

He wanted to ask her if she was still a proper young lady; he wanted to tell her she was beautiful, but he didn't have the nerve. Instead, he asked, "How did you get interested in archaeology?"

"A simple story, really. When I was about ten, I spent a lot of time gardening with my mother. It must have been a spring day on an afternoon like this. The air smells the same—freshly mowed grass, wet leaves. I was digging a bed to plant petunias, rooting around in the mud with my little spade, when I hit something. Not a rock or a twig. At first I thought a piece of wire was tangled on the blade, but it turned out to be a bracelet—small and intricate, but badly twisted and weather-beaten. A bona fide antique, my mother later told me. I couldn't believe that plain old dirt held such surprises, that there really were hidden meanings under the dark, cold ground." The story made Thomas think of the day he found his first flintstone. She flicked a wet leaf off her skirt and continued. "My mother let me keep the bracelet, which I placed on my dresser. Every time I looked at it, I'd fantasize about the woman who lost it. Who was she? What was her life like? Several years later, my parents took me to Greece. We visited Mycenae and Delos. Seeing all those fragments of the past —chipped pottery, broken statues, gold coins—I knew I was hooked. I decided then that I'd grow up to be an archaeologist. I didn't know the term, so I told my folks I wanted to be a treasure hunter."

"I wish it were that simple for me. I don't know what I want to be—especially now. But I know how you felt. When I used to find arrowheads, I'd make up stories about Indian braves and pretend I was out hunting deer." Looking into her soft brown eyes, their heads close together, he had another urge to hug her.

She sat up and regarded him—amused but wary. Maybe she was feeling the same way. But she addressed him in a voice that established a safe distance. "Thomas, perhaps you'll come out to Kampsville. I'd like to show you what we're doing there. You might even want to stay and work for a few weeks this summer—that is, if you can."

"Sounds like fun, but I don't know the first thing about archaeology."

"Most of the diggers aren't professionals. We don't have enough funding, so we rely on high-school and college students to volunteer for extra credit. We need all the help we can get. Strictly a learn-by-doing philosophy." She stood and smoothed her skirt. "Think about it. I'm leaving for Kampsville in a few months. If you come by my house, I'll show you the brochures."

"Did my mother put you up to this, by any chance?"

She gave him a look that communicated prim reproof. "Listen! Your mother and I are definitely not in cahoots. I want you to come."

"Okay. Maybe I will."

She checked her watch. "I really have to go." Together they gathered the remains of their picnic: the empty cans, scraps of cheese, the saltine box and plastic knife.

"If someone found this trash a thousand years from now, I wonder what he'd make of it," Thomas said.

"That's exactly what the new archaeology is all about— trying to figure out simple facts of daily life." Her voice took on a professorial tone again.

"Well, thanks for the lesson, teacher." He hoisted the basket over his shoulder. It was hot now. Her forehead shone with beads of perspiration.

Ana turned to face him, standing so close he could feel her breath on his cheek. "Thomas, it's been a lovely afternoon." He nodded. "My turn to hug you," she said. Her hair smelled of lilacs and wet grass. Then she moved away, half running down Big Bend, turning once to wave and smile. This was the second time he'd watched her hurry off, probably to get home to her little boy, who needed to know the names of things, as he did.

Thomas wanted to hurry somewhere too, but not home. His head was spinning, high on the afternoon and being with Ana. She was gorgeous. Latham and Rafferty would shit purple if they saw her. Then he wondered why he needed to do that—turn the afternoon into a sexual encounter, play Mr. Macho. Hell, why not? He could still have his fantasies. But there was that gnawing feeling inside, forcing him to be more honest with himself.

8

TEN DAYS AFTER Thomas started chemotherapy, his hair began to fall out. Tiny curly strands, then thick clumps sprinkled the couch, pillows, and rugs. The shedding continued well into the following week. He began wearing a fisherman's cap, not ready yet to appear bald in public. Now that it was really happening, Thomas couldn't face his reflection in the mirror. He kept thinking it would stop, but soon a few dark patches were all that was left of his hair. At Sunday-night dinner, his parents tried to avoid the subject. But when he refused to take his hat off at the table, his father started harping at him to get fitted for a wig. They sat glaring at each other across a platter of corn beef and boiled potatoes.

"Time out, you two," said Sylvia. "You look like a couple of stags ready to lock horns. Now eat your supper."

"Then let's drop the subject of my hair, or lack of it," Thomas said crossly.

"Absolutely," said Sylvia. "Sam, have some rye bread."

But Thomas knew his father wouldn't quit. "In your case, the hair will grow back," Sam said, rubbing his own bald head. "If you want to hide your baldness, wear a wig. You're going to make people uncomfortable."

"Who gives a damn what other people think?" Thomas sputtered. He'd seen those puffy faces with their lopsided wigs coming in and out of the treatment center. They didn't fool anybody—crooked, apologetic smiles; crooked, apologetic wigs.

"Well, it's going to be humiliating for you. What do you want to flaunt your illness for? A wig will make you like everybody else . . ." and so on, until Thomas thought he might explode and shove his father's face in the potted fern on the table between them.

"You look like hell," said Sam. "You don't have to go around town looking like hell."

"The truth is, Dad, you're the one who's humiliated. Not me. My son, the freak. All you care about is appearances."

Sam started up again. "You look like one of those Hare Krishna creeps, or Kojak."

"You're the one with the hang-up about hair!" Thomas shouted. "Just because you're old and bald . . ." The words shattered like glass across the room.

"I'm telling you this for your own good. Why do you want to call attention to yourself?"

"It's phony, dammit. This whole disease is disgusting, anyway. The drugs give me the dry heaves, diarrhea, and sores in my mouth. Why do you have to gnaw away at me, too?" Thomas clenched his fingers, his heart racing. They had worked up to a shouting match. His father was used to getting his own way, but not this time. Not this time. "Oh, what's the use." Thomas started to walk out.

"Why don't you consult your friends on the subject?"

wheedled Sam, trying a new tactic. "I haven't seen you spending much time with them lately."

"Oh, so now you're going to ridicule me for not having any friends?" growled Thomas. "Just cut it out. I've really had it with you. Lay off about my hair. Don't push me about my friends. Just get out of my life!"

His father looked as if he'd received a blow. And then he did something that shocked Thomas. He pushed back his chair and stumbled into the living room. Bending over, crumbling on the couch, he started sobbing. His large frame heaved, and he cried in low, broken moans like a whimpering child. Thomas, used to his father's loud outbursts, had never seen him break down before. Not like this.

For the first time, Thomas felt as if he might die. Gasping for breath, he sank down on the couch, his body rigid, as he watched his father weep. Even when his mother hurried over and tried to comfort them, cradling both in her arms, Thomas couldn't let himself go.

Finally, he left his parents alone, slumped together on the couch, their heads bent as if in prayer.

9

ANOTHER BORING WEEKEND to get through, thought Thomas, staring at the ceiling. Eight o'clock. Too early to sleep, and he was feeling nauseated from the injection of platinum he'd received that afternoon. Besides, lately he found himself thrashing all night, trying to ward off nightmares of deadly weapons and carnivorous monsters tearing his body to shreds. Dr. Myerson told him the dreams were a typical reaction to the radiation machine.

"Am I behaving the way other people do, questioning each step, playing 'Doubting Thomas' all the time?" he'd asked.

"You're young and strong. If you had to get cancer in your life, this is the best time. You have more endurance than most of my patients."

But I'm going to do more than endure, thought Thomas, reaching for his marijuana pills on the night table and switching on his stereo. If cancer really was a test of endurance, then he wanted to go beyond his limits. He knew he needed a short-term goal. Ana's suggestion that he work at the dig appealed to him, but he wasn't sure he could handle long hours in the sun doing manual labor. He lay there in a semiconscious state. Marijuana, he'd found, was the only way to relieve the nausea and depression. Neither Valium nor Seconal could do the trick, and he was frightened of getting addicted. Good old Myerson. The only guy at Children's Hospital who could dole out the stuff. He let his body relax to the sounds of steel drums and guitar. Reggae music and marijuana—the perfect combination.

"Smoking my Ganja, feelin' rasty," crooned Rita Marley in her island voice. Floating on jungle music, his spirits were lifting.

In the background, he heard a prolonged whirring, as if someone were ringing a bell, and the next thing he saw was his grandmother in one of her crazy flowered hats at the foot of his bed. He blinked, tried to focus, too stoned to move. "Mein boychik. How's my little prince?" Oh, great! Now he was expected to act sociable.

"High as a kite; fit as a fiddle, Granny." She moved closer.

"You look terrible. What you need is a bowl of beef barley. The girls at the Center made it for you." From somewhere, she magically produced a tureen and plopped herself at his side. "Open up."

His senses heightened from the pill, he reeled from the onslaught, her fleshy arm in his face, the coaxing nasal voice. Thomas loved her, but tonight she was too much for him. "For Chrissake, Grandma. Will you cut that out."

She turned down the record volume. "Such a racket! What kind of singing is that, I ask you? 'Best-dressed chicken in town.' What does that mean?"

"It's you, Granny. You're the best-dressed chickie in town." In her rumpled mustard-colored dress, her canary-yellow hat drooping with flowers and feathers, and her face wrinkled and pinched, she did look like a chicken.

"'That's me. Big Bird. Now be a good boy and drink your soup. I read in the *National Enquirer* that cancer's definitely caused by eating the wrong foods."

"That newspaper's for quacks and gossips," moaned Thomas.

"You must shake off this sickness quickly, before you become like stagnant water. Oy, God, it spreads like gangrene."

"Mother!" Thomas called. "Help! Granny's gone mechuleh." He grabbed her hat and flung it in the air, watching the spinning yellow circle. Several feathers floated down. Sylvia rushed in.

"Enough is enough. I need my beauty rest," Thomas said, giving his mother a desperate look. Turning up the music, he rolled over and covered his head with a pillow.

Sylvia started to steer his grandmother out.

"That boy has always been melancholy," his grandmother declared. "Another number-one cause for cancer. Get well, already, and don't be nasty to your poor old grandmother, who came all the way over to see you."

"Sorry, Granny. Listen, I'll come visit you at the Center soon, and tell your girlfriends thanks for the soup."

Appeased, she blew him a kiss from the doorway. "You're a good boy. Now, Sylvia"—she turned to her daughter as they shuffled off—"my friend Sophie read in the *Digest* that cancer . . ."

Thomas groaned under the pillow. I've got to get out of here, he thought, grimacing into the mattress.

10

THOMAS SAT in the waiting room of the oncology center and tried to concentrate on an article in *Sports Illustrated*. CARDINALS ROUT EXPOS. Baseball season was in full swing. The Cards were ahead by three games, at the top of the National League for a change. "You've got to go as hard as you can as long as you can," said pitcher Steve Mura. Thomas stared at a picture of Keith Hernandez and tried to feel inspired. But his grandmother's pronouncement kept running through his mind. "That boy has always been melancholy." "He eats the wrong food." True, he had a lot of bad moods. He ate junk, too. Was it his fault he had cancer? He'd read somewhere that tuberculosis was the disease of melancholy poets, like Keats. A romantic notion. But there was nothing romantic about cancer. As far as he was concerned, it was in the same vile category as herpes or syphilis. Why did he let his grandmother get to him? She was senile, anyway.

As he nursed his gloomy thoughts, he looked around the room at the other patients, who stared vacantly toward the receptionist's desk. He knew they were all as tense, dreading the inevitable calling of their names. A woman came in with a tall, skinny boy leaning on her. He couldn't have weighed more than sixty pounds. There were no seats left except one next to Thomas, so he offered them his chair. She smiled gratefully. As Thomas moved toward the window ledge, he felt a tug at his pants. He looked down to see a small girl with huge brown eyes, a bonnet covering her head, smiling up at him. She clutched a doll, which was wearing the same blue-checked cap. "Hi. My name's Cynthia. This is Margaret," she said, offering him the doll.

"Hi there." He patted the doll and smiled. "I'm Thomas."

"You're too big to be here," she said gravely and scooted over to her mother. Her eyes darted to the door and back to her mother as she chewed on her nails. He'd seen her before. In fact, he was beginning to be familiar with all the regulars and their parents. Sometimes they talked about their children's treatments, comparing notes. Words like intravenous, cobalt, metastases, and mitoses were bandied about like passwords. They had their own special vocabulary. The simple word "cancer" seemed as ordinary as "mumps," "measles," or "chicken pox." Somehow, they needed the impressive labels. But most of the time they all sat in sympathetic silence. At the beginning, Thomas had hated the association, as if he really didn't belong there. But now he wondered about the children, felt for them each time one stumbled out of the treatment room. Sometimes, one of the mothers would pass around a box of homemade brownies. Everyone knew the recipe included marijuana, even the doctors, but they pretended to look the other way.

"Cynthia Ramos," the secretary called. The little girl grabbed her mother and pressed her head to her sleeve. She bit her lips stubbornly and refused to budge. Two attendants tried to lead her off gently, but she began kicking and screaming.

"Please, love," her mother whispered. "It's going to be all right." But to no avail. Several seconds passed of scuffling and sobbing. "Don't make me go. Please." Her mother shook her head, tears streaming down her face. Then Cynthia sat up straight and slowly disengaged herself from her mother. "Hold Margaret," she whispered. "She doesn't like to see me hurt." Slowly, she walked behind the young attendant. The wails of anguish that soon shot down the halls made Thomas tremble.

"She's had two operations already," her mother told them in a dull voice. "Now chemotherapy."

"What will happen to her?" Thomas asked Dr. Myerson later.

He shook his head. "We're doing what we can, but there's not much hope. Maybe six months at the most."

"Then why make the poor kid suffer through all that pain? Let her die in peace."

"Look, we have to hope we're wrong, that maybe she'll pull through. Every day some researcher comes up with a new cancer treatment. How can we give up on her?" Dr. Myerson sighed and went to the sink to splash cold water on his face. "Believe me, Thomas. I feel badly about Cynthia, about all my patients, but that's the nature of the work we do here. Sometimes, thank God, we're successful." He fiddled with Thomas's chart. "Have you been getting out, doing any exercise? Soccer's off the list, but there's no reason to curtail other activities when you're feeling all right."

"Doc, has my tumor shrunk?" Thomas blurted out. "Am I better?" That's what he needed to know.

"Your X-rays will be taken again in a few weeks," said Dr. Myerson, as he rang for the chemotherapist. First the blood test, then Thomas squeezed his eyes shut as she inserted the syringe and needle into the tubing. Watching the liquid make its way down from the bottle to the tube was worse than feeling the jab.

11

TODAY AS HE LEFT the hospital and waited for the bus, he felt none of the familiar nausea. The dosage had been weaker than usual. Adriamycin didn't catch up with him until the fifth day of the cycle. On these days, Sylvia let him go alone, although she wouldn't allow him to drive himself.

But as soon as the door of the bus clanked shut, he began to be afraid. What if he had to vomit? What if he couldn't get off and fainted in the aisle? A derelict sat near him, smoking. Thomas got a whiff of stale smoke and gagged. This old bum was filling his lungs with poison, and Thomas was the one with cancer. Thomas wouldn't have wanted to change places with him; yet he felt envious, jealous of every healthy body on the bus.

First stop Kingshighway, then Lindell, Wydown, to Hanley. The ride seemed interminable in the lunch-hour traffic. He got off and breathed a sigh of relief. He'd made it. His head cleared as he leaned against the mailbox. No bad side effects today. The sun's heat warmed him, and he noticed for the first time it was a beautiful day. He felt pretty good now. No sense in going home yet. His mother would only tell him to take a nap.

Crossing the road, he wandered in the direction of the local hangout. He took his time, smiling when he saw a squirrel, noting the orange and reds of honeysuckle and roses, smelling the sweet aromas of spring. Maybe Latham and Rafferty would be at their usual booth. He felt like running into them while he was in a good mood. He pulled out his cotton navy cap and put it on.

The odor of greasy hamburgers and the sound of laughter greeted him as he stepped out of warm sunlight into the fan-blown air. Still the same crummy joint. Mr. Edwards (alias "Ptomaine Teddy") lounged behind the counter in his oil-stained apron and scratched his stubby beard. Loretta, his wife, swatted a fly and flipped a meat patty at the same time. Thomas wondered where the fly landed. Two girls bounced in time to "I Wanna Hold Your Hand" blaring from the jukebox. A sign on the door read: "No Dogs Allowed." Someone had crossed out "Dogs" and scrawled "Adults." Rumor had it that Ptomaine Teddy peed in the pickle barrel and Loretta's hamburgers were horsemeat. Still, students at Clayton High would riot if the Health Department closed down the place.

There they were, old Rafferty and the Hulk huddled in the corner, probably discussing baseball strategies. Self-conscious about his limp, he tried to be inconspicuous, but he had to practically elbow his way through the crowd waiting to order. No one paid attention even when he muttered "Excuse me." Locked arms, piles of knapsacks, shuffling bodies—the place was a zoo. He squeezed through and made his way past Rosie Ross and Muff Klein, who were so busy combing their hair and stuffing down french fries that they didn't even say hello. Maybe they didn't recognize him. "A mere shadow of my former beautiful self," Thomas muttered. But Rafferty and the Hulk spotted him and bounded down the aisle.

"Wow! I can't believe it!" "Where have you been hiding?" As if they didn't know. Rafferty's shocking-pink polo shirt and matching socks almost blinded him. The Hulk wore his holey soccer jersey and baggy jeans.

"A welcome sight for sore eyes." Thomas grinned. Pulled into the booth, he found himself besieged with questions. "What's happening?" "Can you still be on the team?" "Are you coming back to school?"

Thomas tried to answer the questions without sounding as if he were on his last legs. Then the conversation switched to the usual bantering. "Hey, look over there." Rafferty pointed to a group of girls in the next booth. "Not so obvious," the Hulk groaned. "See the one in the red Izod with the big tits?" Thomas recognized Penny Slater. "She's hot for me."

"You're nuts," retorted Latham. "She's not hot for anything but her English book." She glanced over, but Thomas avoided her gaze. The talk swirled around Thomas's head. He found it hard to concentrate. His mind strayed elsewhere as he became more aware of a slight burning in his stomach and a taste of gastric juice in his mouth, forewarnings of an attack of nausea. He knew he couldn't stay there much longer. Regarding his friends' faces, he wondered if his discomfort was noticeable. He felt ten years older.

Their talk had little meaning for him. They were discussing tonight's party, but no mention was made of Thomas joining them, as if it was taken for granted that he was out of commission. Then the Hulk leaned over. "Hey, Thomas, are you still with us?" He grabbed Thomas's hat to twirl it in his fingers . . . then stopped, an expression of shock over his face. "Gosh," said Latham sheepishly, handing back the cap. "I'm really sorry."

"It's called alopecia," Thomas stammered in an effort to recover. "Less politely, hair loss from the chemo. The hair will grow back eventually."

There was an awkward silence. Thomas's one thought was getting home and vomiting as soon as possible.

"Look, Thomas. Can we do anything?" "Maybe you could work out with us?" Their faces betrayed a puzzled concern. He knew they meant well, but he'd moved into another world now, a dark world of needles, X-rays, blood tests, and bad dreams, a world they couldn't be expected to understand. Yet he wanted to hold on to their friendship. Their offer to help felt like a lifeline to the normal world.

"Sounds good, thanks. Listen, I'm starting to get a bad reaction from this morning's treatment," Thomas said, "so right now I think I'd better get home before I throw up all over Ptomaine's table." Visibly relieved, as much for Thomas's show of humor as for his departure, his friends accompanied him outside, walking a little behind him, as if he were contagious.

"So long," Thomas said, swinging his hat on his finger and plopping it back on. He tried to saunter off as casually as possible. His stomach was churning, and his hip ached. Only after he had gone around the corner was he aware that someone was following him. When he turned, he found himself facing Penny Slater, who nodded cautiously.

"I wanted to call out," she murmured, "but I wasn't sure how you'd react. Under normal circumstances, you've never been real friendly."

"So these aren't normal circumstances?" he asked in his most ironic voice, aware, after Latham's remarks, that she did have a fairly decent shape. She stood in her stooping pose, wearing a tight Izod and cutoffs. She would probably say the usual "I'm thinking of you" bit, which, coming from people his own age, always made him embarrassed, left him sputtering.

"I just wanted to ask if you needed anything—notes from English class, or books from the library?"

He didn't want to appear rude; still, she had such a sheepish look on her face, he knew she must be feeling sorry for him. So he said gruffly, "I can manage. I don't have to make the work up until next term." He turned to go, then felt guilty for being so abrupt. "Thanks anyway."

She shrugged. "Do you have my number? I could give it to you."

"That's all right," he said, the queasiness threatening to take over. "I've gotta go." He took off down the alley, stopping only once, to pull his cap off and pitch it in a trash can.

12

TWO WEEKS PASSED, but no calls from Latham or Rafferty. He guessed they'd given up on him. He felt lonely. It was the middle of his chemo cycle. No drugs, just rest and recuperation. His energy had returned and he had cabin fever. The ladies at the Center sent over an apple pie when his grandmother learned he'd gotten back his appetite. To amuse himself, he read some trashy novels and planted an herb garden for his mother. Parsley, thyme, rosemary, oregano, and dill. The seeds began to sprout in five days. Some seedlings grew tall and healthy, while others, nurtured by the same sun and soil, sagged and died. He kept watching one spindly parsley plant, its leaves brown at the edges. He'd sprinkle extra water. The stalk would straighten up for a few hours, then grow limp in the afternoon sun. Thomas was determined to save it. Persistence and a will to live—that's what they tell me it takes, he told the drooping stalk. Is it worth the effort, the pathetic plant seemed to ask, straggling in the midst of its healthy brothers. Yes! Now live, dammit!

Thomas decided to call Ana. When she invited him over for dessert and coffee, he accepted eagerly. But by eight o'clock he grew nervous.

He kept putting it off, afraid to face her looking like one of her early Woodland Indians—scalped. It was nearly ten when he arrived at her front door, slumping there, with an apologetic sigh. He stood presenting himself to her like a consolation prize, and she started to put her hands on his shoulders, then hesitated.

He didn't know what to say, especially since Ana seemed bewildered too. Finally, she spoke in a slow voice, as if choosing each word carefully. "Thomas, I have to tell you that my parents were in and out of hospitals for years while I was growing up. I used to fear doctors and nurses. The smell of hospitals still makes me gag, and I've always had a hard time being around sick people."

"Maybe I ought to go home if you can't deal with sick people," he said crossly.

"Wait a minute. What I'm trying to say is that I've tried to get over my fear. Every time Nicky got a cold, I used to panic. I got over it. Please don't leave. Let's take a walk. Then I'll stuff you with the best gooey butter cake you've ever tasted. Compliments of Lake Forest Bakery, of course. I'm not much of a cook." She smiled lamely.

They walked down the driveway, across the grass, and finally to the foot of a large beech tree. She held his elbow. Her grip was firm. "Do you want to sit down? It's so cool tonight."

Not being able to see her features in the dark, he could only guess her expression and had to rely on touch—the hard, firm leg next to his, the steady rhythm of their breathing. He was aware of the grass like sharp needles through the gauzy material of his shirt.

"Look at the sky," she said. "Stars screened in vapor. It will rain by morning. You should come out with me to Kampsville. At this time of year, the fields are covered with wild flowers, and you can walk through them for miles."

"I love the country, too," Thomas said. "I used to take my sleeping bag and camp by the river. It's one of the few places where I feel peace, where that expanse of water against sky reminds me how small and insignificant one person is. I'm like one of those tiny guppies swimming around in the shallow. Nothing is such a big deal then."

"Thomas"—she shifted positions to face him—"I don't see you the way you must see yourself. It's funny, but you remind me of all the boys I used to have crushes on when I was an adolescent."

"What do you mean?"

"Oh, those charming, well-bred boys with their shaggy hair, their Oxford shirts hanging out of their torn khakis, their Top-Siders without socks. They never noticed me."

He laughed. "My shaggy hair's fallen out."

"So I've noticed. We make quite a pair—an old, disheveled academic and a bald teenager." Ana looked at him thoughtfully. "I want to ask you something. Have you been spending any time with kids your own age?"

He raised his eyebrows. "Not really. Besides, you make them look boring."

She laughed. He felt relieved and hoped he'd charmed her into dropping the subject. But she went on. "Seriously, don't you miss your friends?"

"Look," he told her, his voice bitter, "they regard me as some kind of a pariah now. Besides, I've always been a loner. I don't need them."

"You mean, once a loner, always a loner?"

He shrugged.

"Thomas, the question is whether you can grow from this experience, or will you suffer through it in your usual style, as a loner?"

"I don't know," he said slowly.

"Needing other people isn't degrading. You might take advantage of what you think of as a tragedy and learn to extend yourself."

"Do you mind if we change the subject?" He felt fidgety, on edge. Mosquitoes buzzed, and ants crawled over them. They were probably lying on top of a damn anthill.

"Come on," she said, standing up. "I ought to go inside and check on Nicky. He's a light sleeper."

"Look. It's late. I'd better go on home."

"Thomas," Ana said softly, "I don't have many friends, either, people I can talk to. I feel comfortable with you. Can we be friends?"

"Sure," he said, "but promise not to give me any more lectures."

"I'm just a born lecturer," she said. "Every morning, the first thing I say to myself is, 'Are there any questions?'" The way she cocked her head, smiling at her own joke, made him laugh.

"You are a cool lady," he said.

"I'll take that as a compliment."

13

"Either I'm living or dying," he told Dr. Myerson the next day. "I have a right to know."

"You seem very much alive to me," the doctor said, thumping Thomas on the back.

"I know you have conferences with my parents. Why can't I be in on them?"

Myerson shifted his weight and frowned. "Your parents are very concerned, and I need to reassure them from time to time."

"But if you're discussing changes in my treatment schedule or results of blood tests, I shouldn't be left out." Just because he was underage didn't mean he had no say in what happened to him. He didn't like being patronized.

"You're right. It's not fair, but there are times when patients become upset by knowing too many harsh facts. Your parents are trying to spare you."

"I understand that, but from now on I want to make my own decisions about everything. I want to know all the information you have." Thomas circled the room like a caged animal. He hit his fist on the wall. "Dammit, this whole thing's hard enough without feeling there's something I don't know."

Then it was Dr. Myerson's turn to pace back and forth. "All right, Thomas. Shoot," he finally said. "Any questions you have I'll answer, and from now on you'll be in on whatever I discuss with Sam and Sylvia."

"I've read that the drugs leave permanent damage."

"What do you mean?"

"That I might be sterile." He could hardly get the word out.

"It's true that while you're in the process of having chemotherapy in general, conception is less likely, but don't count on it as a contraceptive. You're not taking any of the drugs that cause sterility." Dr. Myerson peered over his spectacles at Thomas. "A lot of my patients feel too lethargic from chemotherapy or self-conscious about hair loss to be much interested in sex."

For the first time, Thomas managed a smile. "Chemo's not affecting my sex drive, just my success rate. But my fantasy life's terrific."

"Have you been getting out with your friends?" Dr. Myerson asked casually, as he rolled up Thomas's sleeve to wrap the tourniquet around his arm.

That same question again. First his father, then Ana, now Dr. Myerson. He wished they'd leave him alone. "A little. I'm not much in the mood to party right now."

"Did I hear 'party,' " said the chemotherapist, carrying in her tray of goodies.

Thomas grimaced as she gave him an injection of adriamycin. "The old killer drug, again," Thomas said, gripping his wrist as the liquid flowed in. A burning sensation. His fingers and toes tingled and itched painfully. The IV system seemed out of focus. He felt woozy and disoriented. "Leave me alone for a while," he told them. Later, when the nurse maneuvered him into a wheelchair and took him out to a cabstand, he felt angry at himself for letting her wheel him out. It was admitting that his body was losing the battle. The sky was black with huge, looming clouds. Then a crack of thunder. Through his haze, the nurse's white dress reminded Thomas of a death shroud against the gray background.

He got home, puked in the holly bush, and barely made it to his room. If this is living, what's it like to be dying, he asked himself. He couldn't bear the suspense of not know-

ing where he stood; yet there was a part of him that didn't
want to find out. He felt suspended, hanging in a void,
living a half-life.

14

GETTING CANCER was bad enough, but developing a crush
on his mother's friend was ridiculous, Thomas thought.
Nevertheless, if Ana Zacharian, professor and divorced
mother of one mysterious child, wanted to maintain a "just
friends" arrangement, Thomas was in no position to
argue. Besides, how does someone his age go about being
buddies with an older woman? Dinner at the Pizza Hut
was out of the question—bowling impossible, lunch at
Ptomaine Teddy's even worse. As he watched the sun rise,
he plotted his next move.

Thomas finally hit on a visit to the Art Museum, where
there was an exhibition of sixteenth-century painting. He
could show off what little he'd memorized in art-history
class; Ana might lecture him on why there were no great
women painters in the Renaissance. Raphael, Da Vinci,
Michelangelo—he prepared a list of names to drop.

His mouth had a terrible metallic taste from the drugs
this morning. Listerine couldn't get rid of it. Six a.m.—too
early to go knocking on Ana's door. He practiced trying to
walk without hobbling, but a sharp pain shot down his leg
every time he straightened it out. He rummaged through
the refrigerator, but nothing looked appetizing. When he

lost his appetite during the last bout with the drugs, he'd dropped about eight pounds. His grandma told him he looked like a cadaver. He forced himself to eat some Bran Flakes. It occurred to him that he ought to set some positive goals for himself, to withstand the next year, other than the obvious task of staying alive. He thought about Ana's remarks, which implied that he might learn something new about himself. Maybe she could inspire him, revive his sense of purpose. He planned to question her about going to the digs. Ancient refuse under a corn field, the ruins of a civilization! A fitting occupation for a complete wreck. Other guys his age might dream of making a million dollars. He had to take life one day at a time.

At ten o'clock, his mother caught him sneaking out the back door. "Aren't you going to bother saying good morning?" she chided. He muttered something about going to the health food store.

"Why don't you wear this?" She handed him Sam's hat, balancing it in front of her as if it were a shield. Her eyes flickered on his face but avoided meeting his. He felt like grabbing the silly houndstooth cap and flinging it on the floor. Instead, he walked out and slammed the door. What a pest she was! If only there were some kind of insecticide, a harmless repellent spray that could keep her away. EAZY OFF: Tough on mothers, yet nice on you.

A small, tousle-haired boy answered Ana's doorbell. Barefoot, he stood eyeing Thomas suspiciously, rubbing his nose with one fist and clutching a ragged security blanket with the other.

"I used to have one of those," Thomas began, "but it was purple." The slight pout turned into a smirk. Nicky looked remarkably like Ana—the same high cheekbones, dark doe eyes, and slender frame. He had a fragile countenance, as if he expected to be abandoned at any minute.

"What happened to your hair?" Nicky demanded in that direct way kids have.

"I guess you're referring to my bald head. It's because my hair's growing down instead of up."

A spark of interest. Nicky's eyes widened. "Won't it get tangled in your brains?"

"Maybe," Thomas answered, smiling. Now Nicky grinned back, satisfied with the exchange.

"I guess you're here to see my mom. She's in the kitchen having a fight with my father. I've got to go to school," he added importantly, as if only grown-ups could afford to pass the day arguing in the kitchen. Nicky, blanket in tow, grabbed his beat-up sneakers and took off toward a red station wagon that had just pulled into the driveway. Thomas felt a sudden pang. He wished he were a six-year-old again, scrambling off to school.

The last thing Thomas wanted to do was run into Ana's husband, so he prepared to exit immediately. But Ana popped her head out of the kitchen door and motioned him inside. He found her scowling into the phone receiver. Dressed in orange and yellow, with her hair pulled back, she resembled a Mayan princess.

"Between classes, housework, and shopping, when do I have time?" she shouted. "Can't you drive Nicky to his Scout meeting for once?" She rolled her eyes at Thomas and stuck out her tongue. "Forget it. I'll manage. But he would like to see you once in a while." Then she gave a resigned sigh and hung up, shaking her head.

"Why don't we go over to the museum," Thomas suggested, as if he had just thought of it.

"I've got two hours before my first class," she said. "I guess I could use a diversion. Nicky's father never fails to upset me."

"Just think of me as your resident court jester," Thomas said. "Come on, let's go immerse ourselves in the Renaissance. Afterwards, I'll treat you to a gourmet lunch of hot-dogs and fries, and you can convince me why I should never get married."

Fighting bumper-to-bumper traffic all the way to the museum, she told him about Nicky's father and how difficult it was to play the role of both parents.

"He seems like a good kid," Thomas said. "A pint-sized version of you. Maybe he'd like to go camping with me one of these days."

At the Art Museum, they found the area crowded and ended up parking near the zoo. Arm in arm, they walked up the hill. He was short of breath by the time they reached the top.

"Thomas, are you all right? Thomas?" she repeated. Embarrassed by his weakness, he lunged ahead without answering.

They strolled through the rooms, shimmering with golden altarpieces, and passed the galleries of English portraits and Impressionist paintings.

"First, I want to see the 'Judgment of Paris.' It's one of my favorite pictures," Ana told him. They walked quickly through the large galleries into the room that held the Northern European paintings. A crowd stood spellbound before a small canvas. Middle-aged women sporting large shoulder bags and sensible shoes, they were obviously a tour group. The guide was lecturing enthusiastically in a booming voice, accompanied by sweeping arm movements.

Thomas felt a twinge of impatience. "Let's go. This woman's a bore."

But Ana pulled away from Thomas and moved closer to the painting: three naked goddesses posed seductively for a young man, who sat dressed in full armor under a tree. She listened attentively to the guide's spiel.

"This painting, which transforms myth into reality, is a

masterpiece in which Lucas Cranach's most refined technique can be seen. Paris is about to award the golden apple to Venus and win for his pains the disastrous love of Helen, thus instigating the Trojan War."

"Give me a break," Thomas muttered, joining Ana behind the group.

"I think what she's saying is fine. A little wordy, but fine."

"The myth depicts a classical theme with charming accuracy," continued the guide, her voice becoming high-pitched, "and makes the characters of this Greek legend come to life before our very eyes."

"I have a question," Thomas blurted. "If the painting depicts the myth so accurately, why is Paris dressed as a sixteenth-century German nobleman?"

There was some shuffling of feet as the group prepared to move on. Ana hurried toward the exit. Without giving the guide a chance to answer, he ran to catch up with her.

"Why did you have to be so rude?" she asked. "Showing off, putting that poor woman down." Ana was half-running, sliding down the marble steps, her eyes dark with anger. "You're really arrogant. We weren't even a part of that group. Why were you trying to make the guide look like an idiot?"

Thomas tried to defend himself across the lobby, down the steps to the street, past parked cars and a stretch of green, all the way across Forest Park Drive until they reached her Honda.

"I'm exhausted," Thomas said, wiping perspiration off his forehead. "Why don't we stop for lunch." Maybe she'd calm down. But she was still stomping around like the Red Queen whacking a croquet ball. And he was the ball.

She confronted him, hands on her hips. "You told me once you felt set apart. Well, even special people observe common rules of behavior. Cancer doesn't make you exempt."

If she had given Thomas a karate chop, thrown him to the ground and stomped on him, it couldn't have felt worse. Maybe she was right. Maybe he did have a superior attitude. But just because he had cancer didn't mean he was going to undergo a complete personality change. He'd always been this way. There was nothing left to say, so he turned and strode off in the opposite direction. But when he reached Art Hill Circle, he knew he couldn't let the day end so badly. Besides, he didn't want to walk all the way home.

So he doubled back. She was unlocking the car door. "I'm sorry. That was stupid of me. Our outing has certainly gotten off to a great start!"

She stood stiffly with her hands on her hips, but her face softened. "Apology accepted. Get in. Let's start over."

While Ana was making lunch, the phone rang. He debated whether or not to answer it. What if it was his mother? Somehow he didn't want her to know he was here. But after the third persistent ring, he picked it up and gave a tentative hello.

The voice on the other end was cool. "Is Mrs. Zacharian there? This is Linsey Gibbs at Childgrove School. Is Nicky home, by any chance?"

"No," he answered. "He's supposed to be at school. What's going on?"

"There was a bit of trouble this morning. Several of the other boys ganged up on him. He actually attacked the biggest one, Frank Darby, and gave the poor lad a bloody nose. He went out of control. We had to tear Nicky away. But when we sent him to the corner to calm himself, he disappeared. We've been searching the premises for an hour. Is this Mr. Zacharian?"

At that point, he handed the phone over to Ana. "This is Mrs. Zacharian," she said quickly. She listened for a moment. "Yes, yes. I'll be right over." She banged down the phone, and they raced out of the house. She backed the car out, narrowly missing a parked Chevy wagon.

Then came a series of garbled questions. Where could he have gone? Would a stranger lure him into his car? A sex maniac, a kidnapper? Would he be so preoccupied that he might cross the streets without noticing the cars? All the while, Thomas kept thinking of his mother, who never got hysterical, who always stayed calm.

"He's probably fine," Thomas offered in a consoling voice. "He'll turn up around dismissal time." He pictured Nicky, clutching his sneakers as he left for school.

The principal was waiting at the switchboard. "Where's my baby?" demanded Ana. Reproachfully statuesque, Mrs. Gibbs fingered her spectacles. "We don't encourage violence at Childgrove to settle disputes, Mrs. Zacharian. I hope when we find Nicky, he's come to his senses." Ana regarded her with hostility. Thomas could see he wouldn't be much help there, so he went to scout around the grounds. First the bike shed, the tree house, finally the parking lot. He peered in the back seat of a jeep, then under a van.

At the far end of the playground rose a group of oak trees. Evenly planted, sedate, they formed a pedantic brown row. Peering down from a branch not eight feet off the ground was a red cherub face. Nicky Zacharian himself.

"Hi, kid," Thomas said casually, strolling in his direction. "What are you doing up there?"

"Hiding," came a muffled reply. "Mrs. Gibbs and Frank Darby are going to kill me."

"I doubt it. The whole school's in a panic looking for you."

"I'm not coming down. The kids hate me."

"Well, you have a right to your opinion," Thomas said slowly. "But even though they're mad at you for giving that big bully a bloody nose, I think the boys probably respect you for trying to defend yourself."

"Do you think so? I'm in big trouble." Nicky shifted his position and let his legs dangle. Thomas could have jumped and pulled him down. But, looking up at him, Thomas felt that they might have traded places. He knew just what Nicky was thinking—the outcast mentality. It takes one to know one, he thought.

"Even though the school tells you guys not to beat each other up," he went on, "sometimes you have to fight back to prove you can win—just for yourself. I've been fighting back myself lately." But he didn't tell Nicky what he was fighting against. "I know your mom's not mad. She's just worried 'cause you're missing. Why don't you come back with me and tell her you're all right?"

After a moment of wrinkling his nose and tugging a lock of hair, Nicky slipped off the tree and landed in Thomas's arms. Thomas tickled him in the ribs and ruffled his hair. They wrestled, rolling on the grass. By the time the two reached the entrance, Nicky was grinning meekly, his sleeve torn, his cheeks chapped raspberry red.

When Ana spotted her son, Thomas knew she wanted to grab and smother him with hugs, but he was glad to see she restrained herself. If Nicky was anything like he'd been as a kid, his mother slobbering all over the place would have embarrassed him. "I love you," she whispered. "I'm glad you're safe and sound." Even Mrs. Gibbs softened. "Thanks, Thomas," Ana said.

In the car going home, Nicky curled up in the backseat and promptly fell asleep. Ana turned to Thomas. "I really appreciate your sensitivity to Nicky. He needs . . ." She broke off. Thomas knew she was thinking of Nicky's father.

"Well, you've seen me at my best and worst today," he told Ana. The way she squeezed his hand, Thomas knew she would remember the best.

15

HE AND NICKY spent the next morning planting a pumpkin patch. At first, Nicky splattered mud with his spade as if he were playing in sand on a beach. "Watch me for a minute," Thomas instructed, crouched uncomfortably in the freshly tilled soil. "Then you'll be able to plant the whole garden yourself."

"That's too easy," complained Nicky, when Thomas dug a hole and patted the seed in. "The pumpkins won't grow by Halloween."

Thomas agreed it was hard to picture a fat, orange pumpkin growing from that small seed. "Just be patient and water it every day. You'll see." Nicky didn't look convinced.

"Oh boy, I must sound just like a parent," Thomas told Ana, who stood watching at the fence. If there was anything he was short on, it was patience. "How do little kids learn to wait?" he asked her.

"I guess by not always getting what they want right away," she said.

"When's Halloween?" asked Nicky in a dubious voice.

"Four months, squirt," said Thomas. "That's sixteen weeks."

"And 112 days," added Ana.

"All those days," groaned Nicky. "Do you promise that we'll get pumpkins?"

Thomas looked over at Ana. She didn't say anything. "I can't promise, but if you do grow some pumpkins to sell for Halloween, won't it be worth it?"

Nicky nodded and grinned. "I'll put them in my red wagon." Soon he was digging away, no doubt imagining his jack-o'-lanterns in every window on the block.

"Words from the wise," said Ana.

"I should take my own advice," said Thomas, easing himself up with a groan. His hip was throbbing again. "Dammit." He rubbed his hand over the knot. It felt as if a steel plate had been inserted in his pelvis. Three months of chemo, and he wasn't sure the tumor had shrunk. It was hard to be patient.

"You hardly limp anymore," observed Ana as he walked toward her.

"I practice a lot," Thomas replied. "Today's X-ray day. I've been having nightmares about it for weeks."

"Come inside and have a glass of lemonade until Sylvia gets here," suggested Ana. "Take a break from your gardening duties."

When his mother showed up right on time, Thomas wanted to hide in the toolshed. All the way to the hospital, she tried to soothe him with amusing stories of his childhood. She kept at it down Route 40, across Kingshighway, and up three levels in the parking garage. "I used to practice the piano for hours when you were just learning to walk. I remember your climbing on the piano bench and perching next to me, watching my fingers move across the keyboard and babbling to the music," she said as they locked the car and headed down the ramp.

"Right now, all I can remember is the doctors' offices you dragged me to for my allergies. I think I even broke out from the detergent you used on my clothes." Today he wasn't in the mood to be a good patient.

His mother turned away and strode quickly into the lobby of Children's Hospital. She tripped over the first step. Thomas grabbed her elbow. "Are you all right?"

She didn't answer. As the elevator door shut, she looked at him and said, "You know something, son. I hurt, too." He shifted his eyes away from her face, concentrating on the numbers lighting up on the register. He wanted to crumple onto the elevator floor and cry, but he gritted his teeth. "Thomas, please don't block me out. If you need to scream or weep, I'm here for you."

He shook his head. He couldn't break down. Not now. Neither of them could handle that. "I'm just scared, Mom, that's all." He closed his eyes and bit his lip.

"Hold on to me for a moment before we get there, will you, son?"

He put his arms around her and squeezed tight until the door slid open on the sixth floor. "I love you," he said.

She nodded.

"Mom, let's go in there and get this over with." His arms stayed around her shoulders as they entered the waiting room.

When Dr. Myerson emerged from his office and pumped his hand, Thomas felt as if he were squeezing a lump of dough. The nurses fluttered like white moths. "Take this young man down to X-ray," Myerson told the prettiest of the bunch. She was small, well rounded, and reeked of some flowery perfume. Thomas figured she was close to his age, but she made him feel like a two-year-old, the way she patted his arm and smiled consolingly.

"My hip's giving me a lot of pain," he said weakly. "Do you think you could help me down these stairs?" When she offered her arm, he let his hand slide down her back and rest on her thigh.

"Hey, watch it," she squealed. "You're not in pain, you're teasing me." For the first time, she looked him in the eye.

"I just wanted to let you know that I'm still alive." He marched determinedly into the X-ray room.

Later, Sylvia sat next to him as if in a stupor. Thomas could feel her anxiety. When Dr. Myerson called them into his office, he didn't feel as cocky as he had with the young nurse. He felt numb. Sylvia clenched his arm.

"The tumor shows no signs of progression," Dr. Myerson began. "In fact, it has shrunk, but there is still evidence of a destructive lesion in the bone."

Staring at the crack in the ceiling, Thomas felt as if he were somewhere between his body, which was slumped in Dr. Myerson's leather chair, and the ceiling with its jagged cracks. He floated there like some repugnant black cloud, the kind that followed bad children around in fairy tales. He was a mass of thickening, gray smoke. If only he could curl his way up to the crack in the ceiling and disappear, just float out of the building and evaporate into St. Louis's polluted summer air. Thomas couldn't move his fingers; like two dead weights, his hands froze in his lap.

"What do we do now?" Sylvia was saying.

"There are two choices. Either we perform another biopsy to be certain, or we use a more radical treatment. A high dose of methotrexate. Either way, you should go back into the hospital." Thomas fantasized running off to Mexico for Laetrile or going to California and joining a positive-thinking encounter group. Drugs, sex, and rock 'n' roll. Wish the disease away with good thoughts, good humor, and good wine.

"Why don't we discuss this with your father," Sylvia suggested weakly.

"I want to try the new treatment," Thomas said, ignoring her pleading look. This time he was determined to make the decision on his own.

"There's one thing I must warn you about," said Dr. Myerson, his face grave. "The dose of methotrexate is lethal. It's a very dangerous treatment. We have to combat the drug with a shot of leucovorin, the antidote. You'll be in the hospital for at least four days, and then the treatment will need to be repeated three weeks later."

Antidote. The word once had a romantic connotation for him. Juliet swallowing the potion for love. Now it filled him with dread. "When do I go?"

"Immediately," Dr. Myerson said. "Today."

16

A ROOM—SMALL, BARE, with a bed, chair, dresser, and washbasin. Shades drawn, dark. He lay there for what seemed like days, slipping in and out of consciousness. The drugs made him sick; the pain-killers, drowsy. All he wanted to do was sleep. Sometimes he was aware of shuffling feet, whispering voices outside his room. Inside, his parents kept a constant vigil. Sometimes he felt his mother's presence in the middle of the night. She stared down at him while he pretended to sleep.

In his drugged state, he wondered if he was losing his mind. Was it being drawn from the top of his head into some deep, black hole? He kept fighting not to let himself sink, not to give in to the pull. First he felt a pressure in his forehead, then it settled in his throat, pulsing and throbbing until he thought he might choke. It moved down to the pit of his stomach, then back up, rising and falling, a swirling dizziness like waves forcing him out to sea. He crawled out of bed and tried to make it to the sink. A wave of nausea forced him back. The phone rang. When he answered, there was a click. It buzzed again. "Is this Peter?" came a voice. "You've got the wrong number," he rasped, hanging up. Bent over, his head in his hands, he rocked back and forth, moaning with the low hum of the air conditioner.

One night he dreamed he was in the midst of some turbulent, hallucinatory violence. His body felt as if it were replaying a war movie—the open trenches, swamps, the smell of rotting leaves, the harsh scent of blood, mistaken identities under his skin's thick surface. His flesh was caving in on itself.

"Do you believe in God?" a voice said. He looked up. A man in a dark suit, holding a Bible, stood over him.

"What do you want? What are you talking about?"

"Pray, keep praying. Don't lose your faith."

"Get out of here," he said. "I don't want your help." He closed his eyes. When he opened them again, he was alone.

He broke out in a rash—on his stomach, his arms, the backs of his legs—as if he'd been stung by a thousand mosquitoes. Was it from the drugs? Nerves? It didn't matter. No position was comfortable. The itching turned to pain, and he couldn't stand it. He rang the buzzer. "I can't take this," he told the nurse. Then all the months of pain and fear seemed to come together, and he started crying. It was as if a floodgate had been opened. And he let himself go, broke down in the arms of a stranger. He shook and sobbed until he couldn't cry any more, while the nurse held him. "It's all right," she said, her voice filled with an unexpected tenderness. And she rubbed all the raw areas on his body with salve and put an ice pack on his forehead. The effect of the salve and the firm pressure of her hands soothed and relaxed him. He felt better.

"I want to hear music," he told his mother. "I want the blinds opened to let the sun in. I want a steak and french fries. I want to go home."

17

THEY SAY MIRRORS don't lie. Thomas hadn't looked at his reflection for a week—not since he'd been out of the hospital. In fact, he'd hardly been out of bed. This morning he determined to make the effort, but the face that greeted him in the glass was almost shrunken, with a grayish cast. He cringed.

August 1. The height of a long, hot summer. Dr. Myerson had informed him that he'd responded well to the methotrexate treatment. The CAT scan and chest X-rays looked clear. "An optimistic sign. You're over the hump now." The drugs were beginning to do their job. Outside his bedroom door, his folks whispered like two conspirators. A timid rap followed.

"Tommy," Sylvia said, "Ana called. Why don't I drive you over there. She'll bring you home." Just like a little kid going over to someone's house to play. But today he needed to get out. He knew his parents could use a break, too. The truth was, they were all sick of each other. He was afraid to emerge from his self-imposed isolation; yet he knew it was time. He'd been thinking about going to Kampsville to excavate—maybe people would be more accepting of his condition there. Ana had invited him, urged him to come. But he hadn't seen her for a while. He wondered if she still wanted him to help out.

"Okay, okay," he answered. "Give me a few minutes to get dressed."

His mother drove him to Ana's in silence. He felt like a lump being deposited on her doorstep.

"Come in," Ana said, opening the door. Sylvia looked at her gratefully. Thomas smiled weakly. Ana's face appeared about to crack.

He knew he looked awful. Suddenly embarrassed, he headed for the garden. "I want to check on the pumpkin patch." From the hallway, he could hear his mother say, "Thank you for inviting him over. He's been languishing in bed all week. This gets him up and out."

"He's good company," Ana said. "He's doing me a favor." Thomas was conscious of how irritated she sounded.

"Please see that he drinks a lot," Sylvia went on. "Orange juice is good for him." Whenever his mother tried to baby him, he felt diminished, as if he had no control over himself. He hated being treated that way in front of Ana. "Let him get well, already. Between Tommy and Sam, I'm up to my neck in masculine aches and pains."

He waited until the front door slammed. Carrying a pitcher of juice, Ana said, "Let's sit down." She stood for a moment looking at him carefully. "Your mother acts as if I'm doing her a favor. You're not a helpless child."

"Look, they see me when I'm down, nauseated from the drugs, lethargic and irritable. When you and I are together, I feel and act differently."

"You never come by when you're feeling sick from the chemo. I've missed you."

"I guess I just want to be with you on the good days."

"How are you feeling now?"

"Better. My blood count's low, so they're delaying the treatment for a month. But it looks like I'm improving."

"Maybe now you ought to get away, take a break," she said. "I'll make the arrangements in Kampsville, and this time I won't take no for an answer."

"You mean it? You think it'll be okay?"

"Absolutely. We need a precocious know-it-all out there. I'll be working in Kampsville myself for a few weeks. But between giving guided tours and finishing my research, I'll be busy."

"What if I collapse, delirious with fever, in the middle of the corn field? Will you promise to save me?"

"Yes, yes. I'll stop whatever I'm doing. I'll descend on you by parachute, on the wings of an eagle, and leap to your rescue." She held out her hand. "Shake on it."

He enveloped her in a hug instead. "Okay, it's a deal."

18

ON A HOT SUNDAY, in late afternoon, Thomas headed out Route 70 for Kampsville. The back seat of the old Corvair was piled with an assortment of things he or his mother felt he couldn't live without: three arrowheads in an old tin cigar box, a bag of melting Snickers, three blank notebooks, a fan, a radio, and $250 worth of new gear. He knew nothing of that part of Illinois or what lay ahead of him. All he had was a letter with a list of directions, equipment, and basic information. He'd repacked his duffel three times, stalled all day, until finally some impulse got him out of the house and on his way. A two-hour drive. Unless I step on it, he thought, I'll be late for the first meeting.

The highway rose and fell away; suburban sprawl gave way to city smokestacks and high-rise buildings until, winding around a bend, he saw the Arch curving high in the distance and the McKinley Bridge suspended, beyond that, across the Mississippi. He kept his radio blaring, the air conditioner turned on high, and tried to space out, but his father's insistent voice kept repeating, "What do you need to leave town for? Why work your ass off in the broiling sun? For what?" Then his mother said, "Maybe it will be too hot." "It's hotter here," he'd retorted, zipping his duffel. She nodded. "Make sure you wear a hat in the sun." "What's the point of archaeology?" his father continued. "Collecting a bunch of old bones and rocks. What good does it do?"

"That's what I hope to find out."

"For Chrissakes," his father finally said, "take care of yourself," and slipped him some extra money.

But Thomas had doubts, too. With his body flabby from lack of exercise, his skin pale and splotchy from the medication, would he be able to keep up with the rest of the group? Would he have to answer a lot of questions about being bald? Would they shy away from him like the rest of his friends when he told them he had cancer? And Ana, would she show up and spend any time with him at all?

Billboards, gas stations, and rest stops spread before him in an endless blur. Twenty miles to Alton, then ten, three. He considered turning around and going home, telling his mother he'd taken a wrong turn or decided to bag the whole thing. But suddenly, as the Corvair barreled over some railroad tracks and shuddered, shooting forward, it was as if he'd been catapulted through time and space and landed on a different planet.

There the river stretched as far as he could see, glistening with sunlight. Barges piled high with coal puffed slowly upstream, casting crooked shadows on the water's dark surface. The landscape was dotted with small wood-framed cottages, and the Illinois bluffs, thick with foliage, rose high to his right like a series of ancient turrets. Then all his nagging fears—St. Louis, worried parents, the hospital waiting room and treatments—disappeared. A sense of peacefulness took over.

He pressed on the accelerator, filled with anticipation. Following the old river road, he drove twenty miles until the highway narrowed, blocked by construction. Traffic was backed up, and he realized he'd never get to Kampsville on time. At Bishop's Landing, Thomas, now regretting his earlier procrastination, decided to cross the river by ferry to avoid the jam-up. The ferry swung around, rumbling across the river. As Thomas stood at the railing, staring down at the rippling water, his stomach started to churn, bringing on another bout of nervousness.

Forty minutes later and twenty minutes late, he parked his car in front of the reconverted drugstore that, according to Ana's letter, served as a meeting room for the archaeology center. He took a deep breath and tried to slip unobtrusively through the door. There were ten people sitting around a long table in front of a blackboard. On the floor were cardboard containers filled with dirt, and sealed cartons lined the metal shelves. No one acknowledged him, although they all glanced up. They were absorbed in a discussion. He kept on his wide-brimmed straw hat and sat down.

"At most sites," said a heavyset man, chewing on tobacco, "what y'all will be lookin' at is garbage. Garbage," he repeated, stretching the word out, his voice a slow, Southern twang. "But if you know how to look at it, you may learn a good deal about the culture." The man was propped on the table, his stubby legs dangling. He reminded Thomas of the television image of an old prospector, with his cowboy hat, Western shirt unbuttoned, silver belt buckle, faded jeans, and dusty cowboy boots. A real hayseed, thought Thomas.

"May I ask what your definition of culture is, Woody?" said a small, dark-haired boy who had his chair tipped back precariously against the wall, his legs propped on the table.

"Well now, Milton," said the man, whom Thomas judged to be about fifty, "culture to some folks might be goin' to the museum or the opera. It's outside the individual. What's your take on it?" A thick gray beard covered most of his features, although the tone of voice and the way he spit tobacco on the floor indicated his amusement.

The boy's chair crashed forward. Thomas thought he might land on the floor, but Milton balanced it, answering in a flat voice that reminded Thomas of a recording: "I guess it might be a shared set of beliefs based on how groups adapt to the environment."

The man nodded. "Well, that's a good textbook explanation. How 'bout an example?"

"We're all sitting here conforming to the convention of how we should behave in a classroom. I don't see anyone standing on his head and belching." Everyone laughed but Thomas, who began to think he was with a bunch of loonies.

"If that example can be seen as cultural, I'm all for it," remarked Woody.

There were only six boys and three girls, all about his age. One girl facing away from him, a thick red braid down her back, looked vaguely familiar. As the discussion continued, Thomas shifted his chair to get a better look at her. But it wasn't until the leader dismissed them by looking at his watch and saying he was ready for a beer that Thomas recognized her. Penny Slater. Oh, brother, that's all I need, he groaned to himself. He'd hoped to leave his past behind here, but there was no way to remain anonymous with Penny in the group.

"Meet you in front of the cafeteria at 7:30 a.m. We're gonna bust our butts out in the field tomorrow, so get a good night's sleep," the man said.

"While you're at the bar, Woody?" one of the guys said affectionately.

Thomas slid down in his seat and tried to avoid Penny, but there she was, moving toward him with that familiar slouch. He flashed back to the day he'd brushed her off in the street, and guessed she wasn't so happy to see him, either.

"I didn't know you were into archaeology," he said, attempting to be civil.

"There's a lot you don't know about me," she said curtly, and went off arm in arm with the rest of the group.

Thomas went out to his car, followed by the boy whom the leader had called Milton. "I'm Schwartz," he said, "Milton. Got change for a quarter?" Thomas shook his head. Milton peered into his car with what Thomas felt was rude curiosity. "Man, are you burdened down with junk. Did you figure 'cause this place is called Kampsville, you were going to camp?" Then he snorted and wandered down the street, bending every now and then to sniff a flower or peer up at the cloudless sky.

Even though Kampsville had only two main streets, it took Thomas ten minutes to figure out on the map where he was staying. He pulled out the letter. "Lodging: The Priest's House, the white wood-frame cottage next to the church parking lot."

He dragged his gear up the rickety steps. Someone was sitting at a round table on the veranda. Thomas couldn't tell it was Milton Schwartz until he was practically on top of him. The table was covered with large glassy rocks and piles of slivers, and Milton was engaged in chipping pieces off with a dark, heavy stone. His black eyes gleamed in concentration, and sweat dripped off his forehead. Thomas had no idea what he was up to. "Having fun?" he asked, for lack of a better question.

Milton handed him a flake. "Feel the middle. Smooth as a baby's butt, but watch the edge. Razor-sharp. Indians were a lot wiser in their use of the environment. Chert wasn't just a type of rock. They could modify it to make a whole lot of tools, or a weapon."

"You mean like this." Thomas pulled a few arrowheads out of his knapsack.

"Hey, where did you get those?" There was a suspicious note in Milton's voice.

"Around here, a long time ago. I used to collect them."

Milton handed them back. "What good is a collection? You stick them in a glass case and forget them. What's more important is to study each flintstone in context with the other artifacts found at the same spot. If you remove them from the site, you'll never . . ."

Not up for a lecture, but curious as to what Milton was doing, Thomas interrupted, "But what are you making them for?"

"Just trying my hand at it. Tools like these can be just as useful today. Or maybe I'll spread a bunch of arrowheads on a site and sell them to tourists." Thomas wrinkled his eyebrows.

Milton chuckled. "Don't look shocked. This town is

crawling with lunatics trying to make a fast buck off the digs. They fake artifacts and sell them, rob graves. Just watch who you're talking to around here."

"What value can two-thousand-year-old garbage have to anyone?" said Thomas.

"Most of it doesn't mean anything, but we've dug out some terrific pots, and you'd be surprised at the vandals who get a kick out of stealing skeleton bones. Listen, don't put down garbage. If we went through our own, we'd learn a hell of a lot about our own culture."

"Sounds fascinating," Thomas said, wondering if Milton had a screw loose.

"Who would you guess eats the best-quality food in our country?" Milton rambled on without waiting for an answer. "Rich folks are the only ones who can afford air food—taco chips and stuff like that. The poor eat healthier."

Thomas didn't agree with him there. His mother had never served junk food—she made it a point to fix fresh vegetables and good meats. She never wasted, either. But he didn't want to start an argument. Not yet, anyway, especially as it looked as if he and Milton were staying in the same place.

"Ask someone how much beer he drinks," continued Milton, warming to his subject, "then look at his trash. He's probably lying through his teeth, but garbage doesn't lie."

"Okay," said Thomas, smiling. "From now on, I'll be careful what I throw away—now that I've got a housemate who lurks around garbage cans." Milton grinned back at him.

It was dark now, and Thomas could hear crickets buzzing and the slow rumble of barges on the river. The sky was so bright with stars that he could spot Saturn and Mars.

"Come upstairs. I'll show you where to bunk down. The

john's way out in back, and the showers are down the street."

"You must be kidding," said Thomas, picturing his own private bathroom as he made his way up dark narrow stairs into a long room bare except for several cots and a heap of dirty clothes. "Should I have brought a Sears, Roebuck portable toilet?"

"This place ain't the Ritz, but it's home," said Milton, grinning at the doorway. "Oh, there's only one light bulb that works, and I've seen bugs crawling across the floor that haven't even been categorized yet." Thomas was considering checking into the nearest Holiday Inn, but didn't want Milton to think he couldn't rough it. He prowled around the small upstairs rooms and discovered a sink and a broken shower stall. Then he collapsed on the cot nearest the window and heaved a long sigh. Milton reappeared with Thomas's fan, which he'd left on the landing. "This will come in handy. When are they delivering your stereo?" Here it comes, thought Thomas, snide rich-kid remarks. But Milton, who reminded Thomas of a chimpanzee, helped Thomas unpack his duffel and plugged in the fan. Later, Milton admitted coming from Evanston, Illinois, where his father was a lawyer and his mother a volunteer at a hospital.

"We have more in common that I thought," Thomas said.

"Woody, the old guy with the beard who directs our dig, says, 'What poor kid's going to spend his summer paying to dig in the dirt?' He complains he has to deal with a bunch of citified brats. But he's a good guy. You can learn a lot from him."

"How did you get into this?" Thomas asked. He was beginning to like Milton, who was more laid back than his friends in St. Louis, not so competitive.

"My grandfather died a few years ago. He and I were

really close. You might say he kind of raised me. Anyway, I was getting into some trouble at school, and for a while I nearly went crazy. So I took off, ran away from home and went out to New Mexico for six months." Thomas wondered if he was making all this up. "Then one afternoon I was exploring a Pueblo site outside of Santa Fe that at first glance looked like a mud-washed desert of humps and depressions. It was really a series of walls and streets—an old village. Other people had been there, because I could see the remains of a campfire. I started digging inside a crumbling adobe hut. And I discovered an ancient water jar decorated with intricate designs. Then a little note slipped out. It said, 'This is part of a living museum. Enjoy this pot, then cover it up for the next person to find.' I thought of my grandfather and all our visits to the Field Museum, how much he respected the relics of the past. It was as if something clicked on in my brain. You might say it was then I discovered archaeology."

"What do you mean?" asked Thomas.

"Well, I thought about how people lived thousands of years ago. Finding that pot gave me a sense of continuity— that somehow God's holding it all together for us—that somewhere my grandpa is watching, waiting—that there's a connection between us that might go on forever." Then Milton switched off the light and climbed into a nearby cot.

"Strange," Thomas said as much to himself as to Milton, "I never thought those arrowheads stuck in the back of my closet would ever mean anything to me again."

Snores from the corner indicated Milton was sleeping. Tired as Thomas was, it was hard to fall asleep. He felt excited, raring to get started, his head filled with questions. Would he like the group? Would they accept him? Could he keep up? He pressed his fist to his forehead. Let this work for me, he pleaded in the darkness.

When he finally drifted off to sleep, he was vaguely aware of shuffling and whisperings in the house as the rest of the group returned and prepared for bed.

19

THOMAS WOKE EARLY. The house was filled with the muffled sounds of sleep—quiet breathing, rustling of bed-clothes, squeaking of squirrels in the rafters. A rooster crowed; a barge puffed down the river. He grabbed a towel and headed for the bathhouse to shower alone. But in the streets, early risers emerged from other dorms and strag-gled in the same direction. Smiles and sympathetic moans were exchanged as they acknowledged the ungodly hour—5 a.m., still dark. The grass glimmered with dew. The mist rose above the Illinois River.

"What time's breakfast?" Thomas asked a bearded man, as they both pushed through the screen door.

"Six sharp, and don't be late. The eggs and bacon are gobbled down so quickly you'll be stuck with last night's stale bread." The shower stalls were in the open. "Just like the army," remarked the man when he noticed Thomas's dismayed look. There Thomas stood, stark naked, with three other guys. His hairless body made him feel exposed, embarrassed. But soaping down, whistling, groaning from the shock of a cold spray, the others seemed not to notice. Thomas was aware that his own body, which he believed to be emaciated and shrunken, was in comparison surpris-ingly fit—long limbs, flat stomach, broad shoulders all intact. Even the swelling on his hip was gone. The man next to him was potbellied and hairy. To his left hunched a scrawny, freckle-faced kid. Just a bunch of nude bodies, each with its own good points, and bad. *Vive la différence*, thought Thomas as someone asked to borrow his soap.

"Sorry I don't have shampoo." Thomas grinned.

The bearded fellow laughed his husky laugh, and they emerged into the gray morning haze. "This your first day?"

Thomas nodded.

"I'm Gentry, supervisor of the Koster dig. Hope to see you out there." They shook hands, and Thomas, refreshed and relieved, found himself looking forward to the day ahead. The side effects from his last treatment had subsided, and he felt terrific, except that he was starving. He wondered if he'd see Ana at breakfast, if she'd show up at all. "I'm a floater," she once told him. "Which means I take visitors from site to site, give them my spiel, and try to raise money."

"Sort of like a Disney World guide?" Thomas had teased. She'd certainly been effective with his mother. And now here he was, involved with her project, too.

After a hearty breakfast of pancakes, crisp bacon, scrambled eggs, and coffee in the noisy cafeteria, Thomas followed Milton outside to the bus. Woody Cook was coaxing them to get their gear and carry the various paraphernalia for the dig. "Pile them in," he shouted. Thomas picked a seat by himself in the back of the bus. He noticed Penny up front and resolved to try to be more friendly. He knew he couldn't pull back, expecting people to come to him. But all the familiar hesitations, coupled with self-consciousness about his baldness, were closing in on him. He felt grateful when Milton flopped down opposite him.

When everyone was settled on the bus, Woody asked, "Did all you city brats go wee-wee?"

"Do you have to be so crude?" yelled Penny, who was stacking her field notes in the first seat.

Woody made a mock formal bow. "Have you ladies and gentlemen done your duty?" Hoots from the rest. "Remember, you're going to be in the middle of a corn field. There's not even a tree." Then Woody squeezed into the driver's seat and started the motor. "Hang on to your hats." The bus lurched forward. A lanky blond named Larry, with a buck-toothed smile and so tall he had to stoop to get on the bus, turned up his ghetto blaster, but all they could hear was static.

"Let's forget the whole thing," someone shouted, "and go to St. Louis." A burst of music, violin and strings, from the radio.

"Can't you turn on some real music?"

"Ain't you got no culture?" asked Woody.

"Not us," was the reply.

"Chicory, my fine feathered friends," said Woody, "is your plant for the day. Blue flower, found on roadsides and used in that great New Orleans coffee. See if you city brats can find it."

"Oh, shut up," said Larry.

Milton promptly stretched out in the backseat and covered his face with a red bandanna. "Look to your right," yelled Woody. Then they were all hanging out the window. Blue flowers grew in clumps on the edge of the highway.

"There's some chicory," pointed Larry, amazed at the discovery.

Thomas was beginning to have fun, exchanging names with the rest of the group. He kept waiting for someone to make a crack about his baldness, but no one seemed to care. He figured it would come out sooner or later.

"Listen to this," said Woody. "If a man can paint eight and a half feet of fence in a day and takes two and a half hours for lunch and three fifteen-minute water breaks, how far would a sparrow have to fall to crack and break a two-by-four? That'll be on your test." Thomas knew that, except for him, the rest of the kids were getting summer-school credit. He resolved to take the test anyway.

"We're all going to bail today," announced Woody, "so prepare to get dirty." A pig grunt from Milton, and groans from the rest.

"I'm psyched to get slimy," announced Penny, turning around. Thomas smiled at her, but she didn't seem to notice.

The bus finally stopped at the edge of a hill surrounded by corn fields—in the distance, the twisting river and rolling foothills.

"Remember, anything can happen," said Woody.

"He repeats that before every dig," Milton remarked.

Lugging round wooden crates, trowels, a water jug, bags, the transit instrument and rulers up a path fringed with tall, leafy weeds and white Queen Anne's lace, the group walked single file. A huge roll of black plastic covered the dig.

"Watch it," said Woody, "so you don't slip and fall in the hole."

Puddles of water filled the center. A steady drizzle began, but not enough for the dig to be called off.

"Blue skies, nothing but blue skies," sang Woody. "Haul out the water." That task was accomplished by a bucket brigade. Bending carefully over the middle puddle, Milton scooped the water and handed the pail to Penny, who passed it down the line, until Thomas pitched the water into the bushes. The whole process took fifteen minutes. The tarp was peeled away to reveal four levels of dirt divided by string and stakes into ten grids.

Digging and measuring the postholes was the task of the day. The area, Thomas learned, was on the edge of the

Koster site, named after the farmer who owned it. It was the remains of a thousand-year-old family dwelling, either from the late Woodland or early Mississippian period of prehistory. Their goal was to dig the postholes, measure the house area, and uncover any bits of flint, pottery, seeds, tools, or charcoal that might give them information about the people who had lived there. To their left was the covered, L-shaped Koster dig. Milton told Thomas it was forty thousand square feet and represented ten thousand years of continuous history. "They've closed it temporarily," Milton said peevishly. "A lot of guff about mud slides."

"Milton, set up the transit," ordered Woody, "and cut the griping."

Thomas found himself off in a corner working alone, even though he had no idea what he was supposed to be doing. Finally, he had to ask for help. Penny was the closest to him. He held up the string and ruler. "I can't figure out how to diagram this square. Where do you start counting from?"

"Are you talking to me?" she said, without looking up.

"Give me a break," he replied. "I guess I do owe you an apology, but as you might have noticed, I'm slightly out of whack these days."

Popping her head out of the hole, she propped her elbows on the dirt ledge and regarded him with raised eyebrows. "All right. I'm sorry you've had a rough time." She crawled toward him and pointed to the first grid. "That's labeled 24 east. Now count down three squares and then start from the other side. I know it's confusing, but . . ."

"Listen," Thomas interrupted, "I just have to admit I'm amazed to find you here. How long have you been doing this?"

"Every summer for three years. I guess I just like digging around in the dirt."

"Seriously . . ."

"I got too old to send to camp, but my folks like to get rid of me in the summer. They heard about this place and figured I couldn't get in much trouble in the middle of nowhere. Turns out I really love the boondocks."

"That's great. Maybe I'll make a good hick, too."

After that, Thomas was caught up in the enthusiasm of the group, many of whom had been to Kampsville before. Penny and the rest explained complicated techniques of measuring and graphing the postholes and rules of conduct at the site. He hoped he wouldn't make too many mistakes.

As if reading his mind, Milton said, "Everyone's a klutz out here the first few times."

Three hours in the sun. The mist cleared and a cool morning dissolved into intense heat. Thomas, bent over his square in his floppy straw hat, looked no different from the rest of the diggers. But after a while the heat started getting to him. Sweat poured down his face, and he thought he might black out.

"Have a swig of water," offered Larry, passing him the canteen. "It takes a few days to get used to the heat."

"Thanks." The water, still ice-cold, revived him. He went back to work, scraping the soil down five centimeters, finding a few pieces of bird bone and rock, not much more. Slow, painstaking, the process seemed endless, searching for a missing link in a mind-boggling chain of events. Then Milton uncovered a long bone.

"Cover it back up," said Woody. "It's not time to dig it out today."

"Every time I find something, you tell me to wait," grumbled Milton.

"It took four months to excavate a dog skeleton," replied Woody. "If we're not careful, a whole square can be ruined."

Penny crouched in the pit, a square about six feet in length. "I'm sure this was the toilet," she announced.

"Why?" asked Woody.

"Well, it's a big square, and there's no debris—no pottery shards or seeds."

"There's a lot of flint chips, though," said Larry, peering over her shoulder.

"If the Indians wiped their butts with flintstones, it's a toilet," laughed Woody. "But don't count on it." Penny tossed her hat in the air.

"It's not what you find," remarked Larry. "It's what you find out."

20

JUST BEFORE LUNCH the next day, Thomas spotted Ana at the site with a group of gabby ladies in tow. It was the first time he'd seen her since he arrived in Kampsville. Thomas was eager to talk to her, but she was surrounded. "The Junior Leaguers," whispered Penny from her hole. "Look like you know what you're doing." Ana smiled over at Thomas and waved, but seemed too busy to talk to him. Somehow he felt snubbed, as if she were ignoring him. Okay, he told himself, she warned me she'd be busy. Don't get in an uproar about it. He began scraping at the soil, determined not to let this ruin his day, yet he felt irritated when she climbed into the jeep and drove away without saying goodbye.

When the sun seemed to be directly overhead, Woody yelled, "Lunch break."

Thomas practically crawled over to the wooden picnic

table. "Man, am I wiped out," he admitted to Milton and Larry.

"Have a delectable Spam sandwich," offered Larry. They munched in silence for a while.

Feeling a need for conversation, Thomas asked, "How did you get interested in archaeology?"

Larry took a swig of water, wiped his mouth, and said, "It's a long story."

"Make it short and sweet," said Milton. "I've heard it at least ten times."

"Come on," said Thomas. "I'm curious."

"Well," Larry began. "My folks collect artifacts from the battlefields of the American Revolution. Every summer we used to take treks around Massachusetts searching for relics—coins, old glass bottles, military buttons, bits of ammunition, stuff like that."

"Is that valuable?" asked Thomas.

"Only to people like my parents," Larry replied. "But there's a network of collectors all over the East."

Larry and Milton looked at Thomas curiously, but Thomas knew they wouldn't pry. He debated with himself, then decided to plunge ahead, to clear the air. "I've been sick most of the summer," he began. "Between chemotherapy and radiation treatments, it's been a bummer. Ana Zacharian's a friend"—he paused—"of the family. She talked me into coming out here. I really needed a break." Talking about cancer wasn't so hard, Thomas realized, because these two guys weren't acting like he was a freak.

"Maybe you ought to change your diet," suggested Milton. "You probably eat too much red meat and foods high in chemical preservatives."

"You ought to get together with my grandmother. She's convinced that matzo-ball soup will cure me."

"Have you ever heard of macrobiotics?" asked Milton.

He wore a turban over his dark hair and a pair of terry-cloth shorts that fit like a diaper. Thomas thought he looked like a swami. "Grains, brown rice, vegetables, beans, and sprouts," said Milton. "That's what your diet should consist of."

"Sounds awful. I'll stick to hotdogs and soda." Thomas laughed.

"Your system sounds imbalanced," said Milton. "I'd watch out if I were you. The human race is fouling up the planets—contaminated food, filth and germs in everything we eat, and waste, the waste is incredible. You never see that in the Indian villages of New Mexico." He rocked on his haunches. "You've got to stop squandering and poisoning yourself."

"Milton's an ecology nut, in case you haven't guessed," said Larry.

"I spent thirty days searching out a hermit in the mountains last winter," continued Milton, whose voice took on the singsong quality of a mystic. "The natives told me he was the wisest man in that part of the country, but when I got to his hut I saw banana peels floating in the stream. Just another waster, I thought. Then I saw the old man, beard flying, race down the hill to catch the peel and bury it in his garden. I lived with him for three weeks, and he taught me. I was ecologically sensitive—harmoniously transformed. Inner freedom, that's what it's all about."

"You are a nut," Thomas said to him.

"That's for sure," added Penny.

Then Milton began massaging Thomas's back, singing:

> *"Rama-Rama-tella-llama*
> *Turquoise blue*
> *I wouldn't fool you*
> *Smell the breeze*
> *Through the trees*

Shiva Shaki Locki Nachi
Oooo Eeee Iiiiiiii———"

—until they began to wrestle and roll, tumbling around in the dirt, laughing and shouting obscenities into the hot, mosquito-filled country air.

"Two o'clock. Back to work," announced Woody.

"Only two more hours of living hell," said Penny, flicking her hair back and grinning at Thomas.

"Just remember, you folks are uncovering a piece of American history," said Woody.

Penny hopped onto a mound of dirt and began reeling off a verse of "God Bless America." Staring at her from behind, Thomas thought: She's a real flake, but I like her.

21

SATURDAY, AFTER THE DIG, Milton suggested they all go on the bluffs for a picnic dinner. Thomas found himself eager to hear Penny's reaction to the idea. For a week he'd worked next to her, and they'd had fun trading wisecracks, getting to know each other. He especially liked watching her bent over in her pit when she wore a halter. He told her so, too.

"Male chauvinist pig," she'd replied, throwing a bucket of mud at him. She'd always had a flip side to her. Now he enjoyed it.

"So, are you coming?" he asked.

"As long as you don't make your famous soybean loaf,"

she said in Milton's direction. "You know, the one that's so harmoniously balanced it's inedible. See you both later."

Thomas decided to find a quiet spot by the river to write his folks a letter. He stretched out on a bench near the bridge. After a long day in the sun, there was something to be said for a peaceful moment in the shade.

Dear Mom and Dad,

Well, here I am in the backwater of America, sweating away in the sun, fooling around in the dirt. Kampsville is one of those don't-blink-or-you'll-miss-it towns. But it has some advantages (I haven't figured out what yet). Seriously, though, it's been one terrific week.

He decided not to tell them how exhausted he felt at the end of each day, that twice dizziness forced him to stop digging. His folks would probably send an ambulance to cart him away.

Mom, Ana is a bigwig around here, and I haven't seen much of her. We managed to have one quick breakfast, and I went to a presentation she gave last night.

Thomas considered those hurried encounters. Ana gulping her coffee, thumbing through various notes and papers, while he made an effort to tell her about his activities. Still, he'd felt kind of proud sitting at the staff table while his friends observed them from a distance.

There are about seventy people working here, students and professionals. The kids on my team are great, and you'll be happy to know your recluse of a son has made a few friends. When I first arrived and saw the leader of my group, an old geezer named

Woody, who looked as if he'd just stepped out of "Gunsmoke," I almost got discouraged. Then I met my roommate, Milton, who wears a turban and eats seaweed. Turns out they're O.K.—better than O.K. There's a girl from my class here, too. The Hulk had a thing for her last year, but I think she might have a thing for me now. It's the way she winks at me (or maybe she has a nervous twitch). I'm writing you on a day like today because things are going well now, and I want you to be glad and not worry.

He scribbled *"I love and miss you"* at the end, signing, *"Your hairless wonder, Thomas. P.S. Dad, I forgot to bring my big M capsules, so don't get any ideas and pop a few. You might get busted."* He posted the letter and headed for a cold shower to wash away the grime. Back at the Priest's House, he threw on his only clean shirt, loose-fitting pants, and no underwear.

"Let the body move freely," advised Milton, "without the constricting pressure of elastic against your skin."

"So be it," said Thomas. Out they strolled to the girls' dorm, where he could see Penny waiting on the steps, her familiar sloping shoulders and cascade of shaggy hair outlined against the green hedges. Gray-green—that was the color of dusk here: emerald leaves, greenish-yellow wheat fields, moss-green river.

"A poraceous, olivaceous place," said Thomas.

"Smaragdine," added Milton, snaking his way through flower beds and low bushes across small but tidy lawns.

Penny loped toward them, wearing a backpack. "Soda and Popsicles," she said. "What have you got?"

"A veritable feast, O goddess of the smorgasbord," Milton announced. "Bean sprouts, soybean loaf on whole wheat, and unsalted cashews."

"Maybe we'd better stop at Kentucky Fried first," she

remarked, linking arms with Thomas and Milton as they trooped up the hill leading to the bluffs. The physical contact with these two new friends lifted Thomas's spirits. He felt comfortable and accepted. A good feeling.

At the highest point of the bluff, which flattened into a ridge and dropped sharply, they could look across the river and over the whole valley. The shiny black tarp which covered the Koster site was visible. Thomas could now understand why that spot had been perfect for generations of Indian dwellers. The land was wide, surrounded by high, protected bluffs. Nearby was a spring that supplied needed water.

"They're filling the whole excavation within the month," lamented Milton. "They'll never find a site with better soil conditions for preserving animal and human remains. I'm positive there's important stuff down there that will be lost."

"But the hole's about thirty-five feet deep now," said Penny. "It's boiling hot down there, and the water level makes it impossible to dig any farther. The supporting walls keep caving in."

"You mean it's dangerous?" asked Thomas.

"So it's a little dangerous," said Milton. "There's still a lost world to uncover."

Thomas wondered what else they could find. A dog skeleton, which proved the Indians had domestic pets, tools, weapons, and pottery, had been excavated to give the researchers years of material to analyze. But Milton, who'd worked on the site for a long time, didn't want to give it up yet.

"If your friend Ana would raise some more money, we could afford the equipment to deal with the water problems," he complained.

"Come on, Milton," said Penny. "Even if the place wasn't stifling and dark as a coal mine, the Kosters need to farm that land. They've put up with the arkies long enough."

Milton scowled.

"What's for supper besides beans?" Thomas asked, trying to distract Milton.

"Surprise!" Penny produced tuna sandwiches, Fritos, and onion dip from the cooler.

"Junk," Milton protested. "Don't you know that cooking is an art form? You need clean, simple food."

"Clean, simple food gives you a clean, simple attitude," said Penny.

"Pass me some beans," said Thomas in a resigned tone. Listening to Milton hold forth all week had begun to affect Thomas. He'd read about some doctor in Philadelphia who'd been cured of cancer by changing to a vegetarian diet. He resolved to stop eating foods with too much fat, cholesterol, or chemicals while he was at Kampsville. Why not give Milton's philosophy a try? What did he have to lose? Thomas realized there was an element of trying to please Milton in all this, but what was wrong with trying to please a friend? Milton had certainly made an effort with him.

"Chew your food slowly, too," advised Milton, producing seaweed salad and a bowl of pale beans. "Americans are always gulping down their meals so they can get back to the TV set."

"There's no possibility of that here in the wilderness," said Penny. "Look up." The orange sky was bleeding into feathered bands of pink.

"The sun will go down soon," said Thomas. "I hope you know your way back." He nibbled on the tasteless seaweed concoction and eyed Penny's sandwich. She winked. The soybean loaf was better—light and crunchy, with the salty flavor of peanuts.

After the meal, Milton announced he needed to meditate, made himself a bed of leaves, curled up, and promptly fell asleep.

"Alone at last," said Thomas to Penny as the white outline of the moon brightened in the sky. Suddenly he felt awkward—just the two of them, without Milton to divert their attention. He'd been aware all evening of his attraction to Penny and had wanted to touch her hand and at the same time avoid her altogether.

Penny looked at him for a long moment. "What are you thinking?" Thomas asked. "I know you want to say something. Go ahead. If it's about my being sick, I'll tell you what you want to know."

"Yes, I guess it's about that. Also, something else. You know I've liked you for a long time. I used to stare at the back of your head in English class while you tried to stay awake but couldn't quite make it. You always ignored me."

Thomas laughed. "How come, when a tall girl stares at me, I always feel short?"

"I guess you just didn't appreciate me then." I do now, he started to tell her, but couldn't. As much as he wanted a girlfriend, someone to care about, how could he admit that now?

"Penny, a penny for your thoughts?"

She didn't respond, just fiddled with her bracelets. "I-I-I can't say it," she finally whispered.

"Hey, I'm not gonna die, if that's what you're thinking. I feel myself getting better. It's almost as if I'm willing myself to live. I don't blame you for wondering. Look, I'm glad we're friends now. Okay?" She nodded. "Come on," he said. "We'd better wake Milton and go back to town. It's getting late."

But as he took her elbow to help her up, she leaned into him, her hair lightly brushing his cheek, the softness of her breast against his arm. She clasped her hand on his neck, a caress so sweet that he felt light-headed. And it seemed the most natural thing in the world to cushion her tightly in his arms. When she tilted her head, he kissed her. They lay back against a nest of pine needles and leaves and held on for a long time, touching slowly and gently, rocking together, soft skin on skin, as darkness closed in and a full moon adjusted itself over the river.

She caressed his head. "The Indians would rename you Moon-Skull."

"Does it bother you?"

"It's just a new part of you. After a week, I'm used to it." And he could tell she meant it.

"Tomorrow I'm abandoning my posthole," he said, "and moving into the water closet with you. Back to back, or belly to belly in the dirt?" She tickled him, and they rolled over, giggling. He sat back, crossing his arms over his head. "There's been such a vacuum in my life. But with that hard-nosed bogeyman peeking over my shoulder waving his cancer stick, I didn't think I could find friends . . . especially a girlfriend."

"You've got me," said Penny, "whether you like it or not. We seem to turn up at the same places."

"A lucky coincidence?" Thomas teased. "Or are you following me again?"

"Maybe," she said. "You know, I saw you a couple of times in St. Louis with Ana." The statement sounded more like a question.

Even now, the mention of Ana's name made him feel a kind of tug. "I met her at a time when I needed a friend. It's because of her I came out here, but she's busy and, well . . ."

"Well, you're just a kid, and she's not?"

"Something like that. But you, Penny Slater, are a kid, so . . ." He kissed her hard. "Today's been the best day of my life, I think. I actually feel poetic," he announced.

"Okay, tell me something poetic, then. I'll alert Mr. Bloughart."

He held her close. "Pennyssimo, you are a leafwork mosaic all lit from within. You are the spell that will drive my demons away. You are . . ."

"Stop," she cried, laughing. "You're going to make me blush." Then they heard the rustling of a branch. Barely visible, Milton Schwartz wavered between two limbs at the top of a scraggly elm tree. Staring up at Milton's body outlined by the moon, his diapered torso and his turbaned head shining in the dark, Thomas remarked to Penny, "He resembles a giant brown-and-white goose. How did he get there?" Milton must have awakened and climbed up while he and Penny were making out, Thomas figured, probably watching us the whole time.

From his roost, Milton spoke in a high-pitched half gabble. "I've died the ninth death of the cat, have seen Satan face to face, have dined in the swine's trough, and descended to the utmost echelon of the pit."

Thomas and Penny scrambled up. Why did he have to wake up now, thought Thomas? But he couldn't help being amused by Milton's sudden appearance. "How was your nap?" asked Penny innocently. "We'd almost given up on you."

"It doesn't look like the two of you missed me at all," said Milton, swinging down like a monkey and landing at their feet.

"To tell you the truth . . ." Penny started, then giggled. "Hey, let's get back before they send a search party after us."

22

THOMAS, MILTON, AND PENNY discovered the Kampsville library. Housed in a ramshackle yellow cottage, the miniature rooms, lined with dusty shelves, were air conditioned and deserted, except for one good-natured librarian, who did needlepoint at the front desk, and a large German shepherd, who dozed on an overstuffed leather chair. Every day after the dig, the three friends rested there, pretending to be deep in research. What they were really doing was giggling and chatting in the back room amid fat volumes and oak desks. Above flickered a brass chandelier with a gauzy cobweb and one light bulb. The furniture was covered with tattered white sheets.

"This place reminds me of Miss Havisham's bedroom," Penny remarked.

The shelves were filled with archaeological data donated by various scholars who had worked at the sites. Milton enjoyed browsing through the stacks, calling out exotic titles. "*Anasazi: Ancient People of the Rock*; *The Land of Poco Tiempo*; and *A Return to Machu Picchu*."

Thomas enjoyed tousling on the sofa in the corner with Penny. "I've been in Kampsville two and a half weeks," Thomas said as they relaxed on the couch, two pairs of legs entwined on the footstool.

"You deserve a medal," said Milton.

"No, we deserve one for putting up with him," said Penny. "He's a walking example of Murphy's Law. If something can go wrong, it will."

"I beg your pardon," protested Thomas. "How was I to know not to lean on that datum post or sit on the edge of the square?"

"What about the day you ran across the site and ripped out the strings around three squares?" said Penny. "It took us all afternoon to measure them again."

"Or remember the time he left his trowel sticking up in the dirt, and one of those tour-group ladies in a safari suit tripped over it?" snorted Milton. They laughed. "Ana was hopping mad."

"Thank goodness she didn't know who did it," said Penny.

Thomas felt odd, talking about Ana that way, as if she were a stranger. "I should write a manual on 'Do's and Don'ts at a Dig,' " Thomas said. All his mistakes had been accompanied by good-natured ribbing. By now, however, he understood the techniques, thanks to Milton's late-night coaching and Penny's on-site prompting. "I couldn't have done it without you."

"You mean the goofs?" asked Penny.

"Seriously, it really feels good to be here." He threw his arms around them. "You guys are great."

"Aw, shucks," said Milton. "At least you're eating decent food now."

"Oh, right, Milton," said Penny. "Bean sprouts and seaweed. Yuck!"

"I feel a lot better, too," Thomas admitted. He hated to think about leaving. There was a new cycle of drugs to look forward to when the month was over. Here, with his friends, he could push back thoughts of dying. But no matter how he tried to deny the cancer, it was always lurking in the back of his mind.

"Your hair's growing," said Penny, rubbing a finger lightly across the stubble on his head.

"It will fall out as soon as I start the treatments again."

"If I shaved my head," asked Milton, "do you think I'd look like Gandhi?"

Here they were, talking easily about his hair loss, as if

being bald was as ordinary as a splinter or a cold. This was possible, he realized, because his friends totally accepted him—baldness, limp, pallor, and all. But then, he accepted Milton's eccentricities, too—actually liked him more for them.

"If only Woody would let me dig out those bones," complained Milton. "I'm sure it's a dog."

"They don't need another dog skeleton," Penny said. "We're just marking time now until they close down the whole site. Besides, the first bone you uncovered looks more like a rabbit leg."

"No way," said Milton. "Woody thinks they've got enough material to categorize, and he doesn't want any more, so he keeps stalling me. Man, I was excavating Koster before he even came to Kampsville. I started working on the seventh level."

"I'd love to get a view of the whole excavation," said Thomas, "but they keep it covered all the time."

"Why don't you ask Ana to give us an extension," suggested Milton slyly.

"Why would she listen to me?" He'd hardly spoken to her for days. He didn't want to admit he missed Ana, felt she'd been avoiding him.

"Come on, Thomas," pleaded Milton. "She has a special interest in you."

"Well, maybe," he said doubtfully. "I'll try."

"Them bones, them bones, them thighbones," sang Milton. When Penny and Thomas joined in a rousing chorus, the librarian ran in and booted them out, back into the thick August air.

23

THE NEXT MORNING it poured. The sky rumbled at dawn, and torrents, like slick sheets of glass, slid down the sloping roof of the Priest's House. Thomas stood on the porch preparing to make a dash to Main Street. Woody called off the dig until the weather cleared.

"Now's your chance to talk to Ana," prodded Milton.

This was a good excuse. Thomas wanted to see Ana anyway.

He found her in the Koster lab, dumping dirt onto a wire screen and straining it to rescue any debris. She looked up and motioned him in. She was wearing denim overalls and had a bandanna around her dark hair.

"You look like a refugee," Thomas said.

"This is my work-detail garb." She smiled, glancing at his cutoff jeans and smudged T-shirt. "I'm cultivating your simplicity."

"We'll always be friends, won't we?" he asked impulsively. He felt they were losing each other. It was bound to happen. He couldn't expect her to drop her work and be with him exclusively in Kampsville. And now there was Penny. But he still felt a longing to pull Ana back, hold on a little while longer.

"Always. Now, can you help me with this?" She pointed to a pile of seeds, nutshells, bones, chert, and pottery shards. "They need to be bagged and labeled—the last of my square at Koster. Next week we fill."

"Milton's upset about that," Thomas said, leaning against the counter and sorting the material into piles.

"There are new places to explore," she said. "It's just not feasible to keep Koster open. A landslide last month almost buried one of Woody's assistants." She put an arm on his shoulder. "Hey, friend, do you still like it here?"

"It's terrific. You were right. I needed to get into something to get out of myself."

"Don't be so hard on yourself. Anyone would feel rotten going through what you have."

"Well, thanks to you, I don't feel so rotten anymore."

"So, ex-rotten kid, how are you doing with your group?"

He could feel his cheeks burn. Should he tell her about Penny? He felt somehow that Ana'd be happy about it. "They're terrific, really."

"I thought you'd like them. That Milton's a real character. Larry's bright, and Penny, well, she's awfully nice, too." The last sentence was accompanied by a raised eyebrow. He nodded.

Then she smiled vaguely and continued pushing the pieces of debris around. Ana's hands moved quickly; she could discern differences in the material at a glance. "Can you tell which one's a pottery shard?"

"All the fragments look alike to me," said Thomas. "Milton and Penny are a whiz at it."

She nodded, as if not quite paying attention. As he watched her, so absorbed in her task that she seemed to have forgotten him, Thomas decided to put in another pitch for Milton. "Ana, is it possible that our group can have an extra week at the site if we work until dusk every day? Milton's convinced we're about to uncover something."

"That's the archaeologist's mirage," she said, shrugging. "Believe me. You kids are always coming up with crazy schemes." The way she tossed out "kids" bothered him. It was her way of cutting him off. When she turned her back and moved to the other side of the lab, he knew she was deliberately creating a space between them.

"Thanks a lot for your encouragement," he called over to her.

"Uh-huh, I recognize that tone." She turned to face him. "Thomas, look, I'm really preoccupied today. I've got to finish this busy work and guide two groups around later. Let's drop this, okay?"

"Okay, okay. If you're busy, you're busy. I'll see you around." He stalked out. She was always "busy."

He was relieved to see Penny and Milton swinging up and down on the seesaw in the park across the street. They were soaked, their hair dripping, clothes glistening from the rain. He hobbled across to join them, climbing up to balance the board with his legs. Face to the downpour, he let the cool water streak down his cheeks. "Rama-Rama-tella-llama, let's drive the rain demon away."

24

FOR TWO DAYS the torrent continued. Water evaporated from the sidewalks and steamed up. Thomas moved through a shimmering screen of mist on his way to the lab. The sewers, clogged with leaves, overflowed down the streets. The trees shook with water; branches and leaves engaged in a showery dance. Only the river, black and choppy, reacted angrily to the turbulence, surging forward, threatening to flood. Milton plashed along next to Thomas and cursed under his breath. "It's raining, it's pouring, Kampsville is boring."

"It's not so boring," Thomas said. He'd spent his free

time with Penny, playing pool and listening to the juke-box at the Circle Café, or hiding out in her dorm room. Milton gave him a knowing look.

The streets were dotted with hooded figures in plastic ponchos, dashing from one house to another. The town, usually empty but for shopping housewives with small children or an occasional farmer in for supplies, was flooded, not only with rain but with arkies looking for something to do.

Woody waited in the lab. "He'll keep you busy," said Thomas to Milton, pointing out the wooden crates heaped with unexamined debris. Milton grumbled when Woody instructed them to clean tools, go over their notes, and map the last corner of the site on a large chart. But Thomas didn't mind a day in the lab. As much as he enjoyed excavating, time spent out of the sweltering sun came as a relief.

Milton popped up and down, tossed his pencil and notes on the floor, and finally stomped out of the lab.

"What's with him?" asked Woody. Thomas shrugged, busying himself with some soil samples.

"Who knows?" Larry said. "He's peculiar anyway. Last night he weaved toward my bed as if in a trance and chanted over my head, 'Everything's swinging, and the sacred one is slowly growing a body.'"

"The kid's always restless when he ain't mucking about in a miserable foot of dirt," said Woody. "But there's more to this business than digging. You all have got to know the rules and keep up with the research."

"Easy for him to say," Penny whispered to Thomas. "He's here digging all year. Let's go outside and see what's happened to Milton."

They found him on the steps. The rain had become a light drizzle.

"They're going to fill in a couple of days whether the

rain stops or not," Milton said, his features twisted into a frown.

"So we'll start on another site," offered Penny.

"But all we can manage is to clear a space before the session's over and we go home. Some other group will find the good stuff," retorted Milton. "We should go to the site now. The rain's stopped."

"I don't know," Thomas said doubtfully.

"I've got good vibes about 'them thighbones,' " intoned Milton.

"It's too sloppy and wet," replied Penny, uncurling her long body from the steps and standing up.

"But the sun's coming out," persisted Milton. "We can take a last look in the central core."

"It would be like a reflector oven thirty feet down," she said. "The temperature's at least 120 degrees. The sun bounces off the walls, and there's no air to breathe."

"Not today," said Milton, perking up.

"Maybe you're right," admitted Thomas. "But Ana told me there's a danger of landslides."

Milton's head was bobbing, a gleam in his eyes. "I think it's worth a try."

"How will we get out there?" asked Thomas. They'd moved into a huddle, heads close together like three witches concocting a brew.

Milton pointed to the jeep parked in the alley. "I'll bet Woody left his keys on the dash."

Penny shook her head and sucked in her breath. "The area's off-limits. We could get in big trouble. Not to mention stealing a car."

But Thomas and Milton were already moving toward the shed, where some equipment was stored. As Thomas hesitated at the door, he caught sight of Ana in front of the office greeting some people. "Hi, kids," she called out, spotting him, too. Then she turned away. Her words rang in his ears: "You kids are always coming up with crazy schemes." I'll show her who's a kid, he thought, pushing away his doubts and ramming through the door.

Within seconds, they'd gathered trowels and buckets and a coil of thick rope.

"Watch the street," said Milton. "When it's clear, we'll hop in the jeep and take off."

Thomas's hands started to perspire, his heart raced. What the hell, he thought, I've been courting death for months. What more can happen to me?

"You guys are complete maniacs," hissed Penny, "but I'm not going to let you go without me."

"Okay. Let's move it." Thomas hopped awkwardly off the landing and lunged toward the alley. Milton and Penny were right behind.

"Let's get our butts out to Koster on the double," said Milton, hoisting himself into the jeep. "I'll drive." He shifted into first, popped the clutch, and the jeep shot forward. With the wind blowing in their faces, they headed down the highway. The distance from the bridge to the back road seemed like a thousand miles to Thomas, who felt pressure building in his head, perspiration running down his arms. Even the nerves in his fingers and toes tingled.

He reached back and grabbed Penny's hand. She leaned over and threw her arms around his shoulders. "We're like Bonnie and Clyde." Her laugh was high-pitched, shrill. He knew she was scared, too.

25

BEFORE THE JEEP came to a complete stop at the edge of the field, Thomas jumped out, groaning with pain as he landed on his bad leg. Penny and Milton raced up the path, with Thomas limping behind.

"Oh, damn," called Milton at the top. "The tarp's too heavy to pull all the way back. There must be at least twenty-five tires holding it down."

"Listen, Milton," said Thomas, "we can pull back the edge, extend a ladder, and climb in."

"Too dangerous," said Penny. "The tarp's so filled with water it will overflow right into the hole."

"We can't turn back now," said Milton. "Besides, give me a rope and I swing like a monkey. Once I get in, I'll be fine."

They managed to bail enough water to roll back a corner of the cover and divert the deep puddle onto the other side. They could see the first terrace, but water weight had pushed the tarp so low that the rest of the site was hidden.

"Give me a flashlight," said Milton. "I'll ease in and take a look."

"All right, but don't go without me." But before Thomas could stop him, Milton scrambled down the five-foot dirt ledge. "Throw in the rope," he called.

Thomas got on his knees to peer in. Without waiting, Milton was crawling into the darkness of the pit. "Hey, wait for me!" But Milton moved out of sight. By the time Thomas reached the second level, Milton was descending the ladder. Spread about in the muck were rocks and pottery shards. Even with a flashlight, the hole was dark, and there was no way to know where the solid areas were. One false step and Thomas could slip. The ledges extended like deep steps, eleven levels. A makeshift ladder of rope and wood lengthened into the deepest trench. Milton's dark figure disappeared under the bulge of the tarp. Thomas could hear him gasping for breath. "What's going on?" he yelled.

"Stay back," Milton yelled back. "The walls are too slick. I have to climb out."

"For God's sakes, hurry," Thomas called. The sides were starting to crumble around him, and water was seeping through the mud cracks. Thomas could barely see Milton struggling toward him. Milton's arms and legs seemed all coiled and twined together as he tried to manipulate the rope and pull himself up. Dizzy with fear, Thomas leaned against the muddy wall.

"I can feel the mud sliding down around me," Milton called in a hoarse whisper. "I can't move."

Thomas leaned over. "Try and grab my hand." Milton reached up, but his foot slipped. For a split second, his mouth opened with surprise as his head jolted and he met Thomas's eyes. Then he tumbled over, the mud caving in around him. Rubber tires bounced and rolled against the side of the tarp as dirt and water splattered around Thomas. A hysterical cry forced its way up from deep in Thomas's gut. Above, he could hear Penny's scream, a vibrating echo of his own. Below, Milton lay buried in debris.

26

THE NEXT TIME Thomas saw Milton Schwartz, he was lying in a bed at Children's Hospital, his body swathed in bandages, his legs in traction. Tubes projected through tape, and containers of plasma and liquid formed a backdrop behind him. Visible only were Milton's black, piercing eyes, a thin slit for his mouth, and several fingers of his right hand. Milton struggled to speak. Even through the bandages there was a trace of the old singsong as he whispered, "Anything can happen. Don't give up." Then he nodded off again.

Thomas sat at his side and sobbed until the nurse took his arm gently and led him out. His head was filled with prayers, pleas to God for Milton that he'd never been able to express for himself. And then, dimly aware of the groans coming from the wards and the sharp antiseptic odor pervading the dingy halls, he limped down the corridor past X-ray and the nurses' station and into the familiar elevator. Thomas knew he needed to go home. As he pushed the revolving door, Ana was rushing in the opposite way. Through the glass and his blurred vision, her face looked distorted, swollen. When he doubled back and stood facing her, he realized she'd been crying, too.

"Thank God you got him out," she said. "Is he going to be all right?"

"I don't know."

"What about you?"

"I don't know that, either. Right now I'm just numb."

"Let's sit down." She steered him to an alcove near the reception desk. "Why?" she asked.

"It was crazy," he said, "I don't know what we were trying to prove. I keep fighting these impossible battles."

"More dragons?" she asked quietly.

He nodded.

"Milton's a fighter, too," she said.

They sat silently. Finally, she said, "I'm leaving St. Louis."

"What?" He shook his head in surprise.

"Nicky and I are going to Albuquerque. I've been offered a post at the University of New Mexico. I can finish my dissertation there."

"Good luck," he said dully. Why hadn't she mentioned this before?

"Thomas, I haven't taken our friendship lightly. Don't cut me off. Despite what happened at Kampsville, you did well there."

"Oh, yeah, just great. They'll never let me go back."

"You didn't destroy the site. It was going to be shut down anyway. You were overzealous. You broke the rules and learned the hard way."

"All this time, I've been feeling sorry for myself, figuring I was going to die, and then Milton's the one who gets hit."

"Thomas, we're all vulnerable. No one's exempt. The accident happened. It wasn't your fault. You've come a long way these last months. Don't negate that."

"For the first time since I've been sick, I felt in control. I can't lose it now"—for Milton's sake as well as my own, he thought.

"You need time to sort out your feelings," she said.

"My feelings?" he repeated. "I feel as if my life's been moving through a series of disasters. Then suddenly a miracle happens, totally unexpected, like seeing a shooting star. I grab for it. That's how I feel about you—about

Kampsville and Penny and Milton. You're the gold rings on the merry-go-round—gifts that I've gotten by luck that I have to give back."

"You don't have to give back anything. You don't borrow friendships. You, Milton, and Penny will be a team again." But he knew nothing would ever be the same. She moved to face him. "Will you keep in touch? Write to me?"

"Yes. Hey, thanks for being my friend." He touched her hand lightly and, in doing so, felt the heavy weight of the day's events lift and pass through his fingertips. Breathing out, giving in to a sense of weightlessness, he squeezed his eyes shut and willed Milton to live as he had willed himself to live. The light in the room shifted slightly, as if the sun had chosen that moment to make a quick, dazzling appearance. Then they were immersed again in the late-afternoon shadows.

27

"ABOUT A HUNDRED YEARS AGO (at least, it feels that way now), Dr. Myerson suggested I keep a journal. I was in such bad shape then, he figured I needed an outlet. The only time I took his advice was when my friend Milton lay unconscious in the hospital. I remember feeling bitter and scared and sorry for myself, stretched out in a lawn chair, swatting flies. That was a year ago. Tomorrow I leave for my freshman year at Dartmouth, and there are some things I need to get off my chest before I go.

"I guess the first thing has to do with Milton. He's amazing! One day, that monkey man popped up in his bed and started complaining. His stitches itched, he had a craving for seaweed, and he wanted out of the hospital as soon as possible. Last summer he turned up at Kampsville on crutches, still spouting his mystical aphorisms, but sporting a punk haircut. Of course, it wasn't as simple as all that. What's important is that Milton made it and we're still friends.

"As for me, the day Dr. Myerson refused to refill my prescription for marijuana, I figured I must be getting better. In August, I finished chemo. It's been nineteen months. My hair's grown back, so I'm no longer the bald wonder of Clayton High. When I gained fifteen pounds, Granny told me I must be eating the right foods. If she only knew I'm hooked on rice and grains, she'd descend on me with the Young-at-Hearts Club ladies and force-feed me knishes.

"Every six months, I'll go back to the oncology center for blood tests and bone scans. Other than that, I can kiss that place goodbye, forever, I hope. Dr. Myerson says it takes five years without a recurrence before I can consider myself completely cured, but I'm optimistic. I even sent postcards to my friends, announcing: 'Thomas Newman's alive and well and living in St. Louis.'

"Sometimes I wonder how I managed to survive. So many don't. When Cynthia, the little girl from the clinic, died last May, the regulars sat around the waiting room and tried to pretend we didn't know. Too hard to talk about it, but there was no way to avoid thinking: It might happen to me. But not yet, not yet. What had we done to get through those awful months? We had to change our lives. We had to keep moving, so the depression didn't sink down. Some of us started swimming or gardening or throwing clay pots. One guy I met ran in the Boston Marathon. I had to immerse myself into an activity right then and there, to learn to live in the present. It doesn't help to fantasize, because how can you plan ahead when you have cancer? Working at Kampsville helped get my mind off my troubles, gave me a chance to be on my own.

"When Milton fell into the pit, I realized how vulnerable all of us are. As Ana once told me, no one is exempt. We all take our chances. I guess I've taken my big one. After this, maybe life will be easy. Probably not.

"Even from New Mexico, Ana still gives me lectures. I received a letter from her yesterday.

> *Nicky and I planted a garden this summer—not an easy task with sandy soil and hot sun. Even so, the pumpkin stalks survive. We bedded them down with mulch, and Nicky waters them faithfully—per your instructions . . .*
>
> *How well I remember that summer morning in St. Louis when you and Nicky sprawled side by side to plant pumpkin seeds. How fragile you must have felt then. Did you wonder if you'd be around to see the pumpkins grow and eventually find their way to Nicky's red wagon and our neighbors' doorsteps for Halloween? Now I see you strong and sturdy as those plants, ready for places I can only imagine. Bright with new life, you are not where I left you. Be like a ball of yarn unwinding—an unloosened spirit; there is a thread that joins us together.*

"She's a bright image that will always shine in my mind.

"And Penny Slater—she's still my best friend. We hung out together all year at school. When my hair grew back, she pretended to miss my 'moon-skull,' but I can tell when girls flirt with me, she loves it. Penny and I spent the summer at Kampsville, supervising some junior-high kids.

Hectic, but fun. Woody sat Milton, Penny, and me down and gave us a speech about following the rules: 'Stop behaving like a bunch of "durn fools." ' But we were back in business again. Ana was right.

"When I came home from Kampsville, my father dragged me to Brooks Brothers. He practically bought out the store. I pretended to be more thrilled with our hotdog lunch on the riverfront, but I couldn't wait to try on my blue blazer. Later, parading around for my mother, I must have checked myself out in the mirror a hundred times.

"What have I learned? It's too simple to make a list: 'Things I learned from cancer.' To stay away from black holes, older women, and seaweed sandwiches? I'm not ready to make a serious list yet. It's naïve to think that I'll ever come to a single conclusion.

"Every once in a while, I get a cramp in my arms or legs. Then I get bummed out, scared I've got cancer again. Two weeks ago, my arm started aching. Out of pure panic, I broke up with Penny and avoided my mother for three days. Finally, I ran back to the hospital for X-rays. Turned out to be a false alarm. But I can't forget. It's under my skin, the stuff that goes on inside of me.

"One night not long ago, Penny and I went back to the bluff overlooking the Koster site, which is now filled with earth, an ordinary grain field again. It's strange to consider that, for over ten thousand years, people came, lived their lives, and disappeared. Yet things remain even when we think they don't. Because of what Ana and Woody and hundreds of students like me have found there, scientists believe the remains of many other cultures lie waiting to be uncovered. If this is true, Koster could be the beginning, not the end. That's the way I feel about my life, too."